A Damaged Girl

Discard

W9-BTO-951

Discard

A Damaged Girl

Travis Hunter

www.urbanbooks.net

Urban Books, LLC
300 Farmingdale Road, N.Y.-Route 109
Farmingdale, NY 11735

ISBN 13: 978-1-64556-511-6
EBOOK ISBN: 978-1-64556-513-0

First Trade Paperback Printing July 2023
Printed in the United States of America

10 9 8 7 6 5 4 3 2 1

Distributed by Kensington Publishing Corp.
Submit Orders to:
Customer Service
400 Hahn Road
Westminster, MD 21157-4627
Phone: 1-800-733-3000
Fax: 1-800-659-2436

Prologue

Zola Zaire closed her eyes and prepared for impact as the cold granite countertop rushed up and smacked her in the face. Her attacker, the man who claimed he loved her, had her by the neck and was dragging her up and down the kitchen counter, knocking down dishes, glasses, and canisters along the way.

What has come over him? she wondered as he growled like a wild animal then lifted her up and threw her headfirst into the stainless steel refrigerator door.

"I'm so sorry, but I have to do this," Andre said. "This is gonna hurt me more than it's gonna hurt you, but it has to be done. Besides, you must've lost your damn mind. Don't you ever go snooping your ghetto nose where it doesn't belong," her fiancé snapped as he continued his assault.

Andre lifted her 130-pound, five-foot-three-inch frame off the floor and over his head and slammed her down onto the hard travertine floor. She felt her head hit the unforgiving stone and immediately started losing consciousness.

"If you ever try to get slick with me again," he said, "I'll beat you until you beg me to kill you. And trust me when I say I will oblige," Andre said with a sly smile as he pulled her back to her feet. He seemed to be enjoying the power he wielded over Zola. He held her face in his hands and looked deep into her barely open eyes.

"Aww, look at you. You can't take the pain? Well, we have to build up your tolerance level," he said as he slapped her hard and pulled her into the living room. "Open them eyes and tell me you love me."

Zola was vacillating between here and the afterlife. She couldn't say anything, but she realized that this had to be what dying felt like. She could literally feel the life leaving her body as what little strength she had left her body. She was going to die. She knew it because she felt her bladder release as she became weaker and weaker by the second.

Then there it was: the white light. She had heard people with near-death experiences speak of a white light but never thought that she would be seeing it, especially not at the age of 27. There was a tall man with skin the prettiest color of bronze she had ever seen. He had curly hair and a beard that hung well below his chest. His eyes were very pleasant and inviting. The man was wearing a white robe and holding a small white dog in his arms. He smiled at her and motioned with his free hand for her to come with him. She was standing on a long dirt road alone, naked as the day she was born but feeling no shame.

The man motioned again, but she couldn't move. Something about him told her that she would be safe with him, and she wanted to go with him, but she couldn't move. The man took a step toward her and reached out his hand. His hands were huge yet welcoming, but she couldn't move her feet. She looked down to see what was stopping her, and her feet were stuck in the earth up to her ankles. The man looked down at her feet and blew an easy breath, and her feet were free. He motioned again, but before she could move, the dog started barking, and the man looked at the animal and smiled. He waved a hand at Zola, then walked away. Zola called out to him, but he and the little dog were gone, and so was the white light.

She was back, and Andre was still staring at her with his hands wrapped around her neck. When she opened her eyes, he released her and smiled.

"Glad to have you back," he said before throwing her face down over the back of the sofa. He ripped her dress off and removed his pants. He approached his beaten woman, rubbed his hand across her exposed buttocks, leaned over her so that his chest was on her back, and whispered in her ear, "You'd be such a good wife. It's too bad I have to kill you."

Chapter 1

Ian DeMarco was sweating from every pore in his body. His mocha brown skin glistened like a crystal in the frigid air of Stone Mountain Park. He could see his destination ahead and was headed for it with everything he had. Huffing and puffing, he refused to stop. He had to run. Running had always cleared his mind, but it wasn't doing the trick today. He called in to work and took a personal day because he knew he wouldn't be any good. So here he was running around a big mountain with a bunch of white men carved into its side. He had already done almost five miles, yet he still couldn't get last night's crazy episode out of his head.

His heart was threatening to beat its way out of his chest as he gripped the handles of the stroller he was pushing. The pain was kicking in. That was a good thing. Anything was a welcome relief from the images floating around his head. He had settled his mind to focus only on his legs and feet. He was determined to make it to the finish line and force the crazy thoughts from his head.

What was I thinking about? Why didn't I just call the police?

The police? Are you kidding me? Who do you think you are? Don't you know who you are?

"Yeah, I know who I am," he heard himself say.

Ian was coming up on the point where he started running forty-five minutes ago. Five miles were in the books, and his thoughts never really left last night's drama.

Ian slowed down and walked at a brisk pace to cool down. A few minutes later he stopped altogether and reached into the back of the baby's stroller. He grabbed a bottle of water, removed the cap, and placed it to his lips. Downing the entire contents of the twelve-ounce bottle in one big gulp, he allowed two more joggers to pass, and then he walked over and tossed the empty plastic bottle into the recycling bin. He turned back and went to the front of the stroller. He leaned down and smiled.

"What's up, little buddy?"

His smile was met by two sleepy eyes. "Hi, Daddy," Christian, his 4-year-old son, said. "I wanna get out and walk."

Ian unbuckled the seat straps and lifted his son out and onto the pavement. He watched as his son's little legs took off running.

"I'm never gonna leave you, li'l man," he said quietly. "I will not let that happen. I cannot let that happen."

"I want to play with my ball, Daddy," Christian said with a wide-eyed smile. His innocent face made his father's heart hurt even more. The little boy had no idea what he had already been through and lost.

"Go ahead, but don't kick it in the lake like you did last week," Ian said.

"Okay," Christian said. He ran back to where his dad was standing and reached into the bottom of the stroller and pulled out his basketball. He smiled at his dad, then started dribbling the ball with his left hand. He was pretty good for a 4-year-old.

Ian smiled and rubbed his son's head. He couldn't imagine life without him, yet he couldn't shake the vision of him standing in a crowded courtroom, fitted in a striped prison outfit, two hulking guards on either side of him as the judge handed down his sentence. He could see the image of Christian crying and reaching out for his father while the judge slammed down his gavel and ordered the guards to take him away from his son. He forced the damning thoughts from his head and tried to think of a more pleasant time. He was looking forward to the cruise that he and Christian would be taking in the next two weeks. They would be leaving the cold Georgia winter for the hot sun and sands of Aruba. He could see them out on the water now, but just as quick as he smiled, the vision of him committing a crime that would ship him away came roaring back and sent a bone-chilling fear down his spine and wouldn't allow him to even have that moment of tranquility.

Ian was the father of two beautiful children he loved very much. Brianna and Christian were his world, but now only Christian existed in it. His beautiful wife, Tasha, and his lovely daughter, Brianna, were no longer on God's green earth, and they died because someone felt that they weren't getting their share of the almighty dollar. Money was necessary, but after losing his family because of it, Ian made a point to use as little of it as possible. His wife's and daughter's lives were cut short three years ago, but to him it felt like yesterday. There wasn't a day that went by that Ian didn't relive the night that changed him forever.

Christmas was always a special time in the DeMarco household. From as far back as Ian could remember, his father, Colin DeMarco, insisted on everybody being home and together as a family.

It was the day after Christmas, and Ian and Tasha loaded up the kids to meet his family for their annual family bowl-off. Colin was a busy businessman, but Christmastime was always reserved for his family, and he made sure to maximize his time with his kids and grandkids. This was the time of year that recharged him for the rest of the year. And for a man who did so much for everyone, especially his family, it was hard to deny his request to make themselves and their families available for the DeMarco family bowling night. This ritual went on every year, and it was always the day after Christmas.

The bowling alley was crowded with people who were home for the holidays. The DeMarcos had rented six lanes, and all of them were filled with family members or people who worked for the DeMarcos, whom his father always treated like family. It was a festive atmosphere, and Ian was as happy as he'd ever been. His mother, Lidia, the family matriarch, was smiling and enjoying watching her grandkids play. She chuckled when one of the small ones bowled the ball between his legs and made a strike. Ian's brother, Malcolm, and older sister, Andrea, were arguing about something—a habit that started when they were kids and carried over into their adult years.

"Stop cheating, Malcolm," Andrea said in her high-pitched voice. "You can't ever play fair."

"How do you cheat in bowling, Andrea?" Malcolm responded.

"You're stepping over the line. That's scratching," she said.

"Girl, I ain't that good. I can walk halfway down the lane and still miss eight out of ten. You just mad because you're losing. Again."

"If you followed the rules, I wouldn't be losing," Andrea said.

"Daddy, please tell her to shut up," Malcolm said.

Colin shook his head and rocked his 3-year-old granddaughter Brianna on his lap. "I'm not getting in that one," Colin said.

Ian was changing Christian's diaper on the table in front of everybody and frowning at the smell of his son's boo-boo.

"Man," Kenny, Andrea's husband and the family comedian, yelled, "please take that li'l rascal in the bathroom like right now. What you got in that bottle he's sucking on, a chitterling smoothie?"

Ian laughed and continued changing his son. He looked over at his father, and he seemed like the happiest man in the world. Family had always been the most important thing in the world to him, and there was never anything he wouldn't do to make sure his people were well taken care of.

Colin DeMarco was one of the oldest black millionaires in Atlanta, Georgia. He owned over twenty-seven Quick Trip gas stations and owned a stake in a Texas oil field. Although his businesses brought in large sums of money yearly, they were all started with funds he obtained in his previous life as an underworld mafia figure. That was a part of his life very few people knew about. The gas stations and oil field were all he focused on these days, but there were people in that previous life who felt cheated. Police officers, hit men, and wicked women were all used at one time or another to try to bring down the great Colin DeMarco, but they all failed, and they all paid a heavy price for coming at him. Because at the end of the day, suits and ties aside, Colin DeMarco was a gangster. And he wasn't just any gangster. He was *the* gangster. He took meetings with very important people, mayors, governors, and he even had a picture in his office with former president George Herbert Walker Bush. To most people, Colin DeMarco was a very important man, but to some he was just a lucky nigga who got too big for his britches. Those enemies kept him on edge because he knew there were some people who wouldn't rest until he was resting in peace. Whenever Colin was out in public, he took all the necessary precautions, which explained the inconspicuous-looking bodyguards peppered throughout the bowling alley.

The night was going great. Balls were hitting pins, people were laughing, beer was being poured by the pitcher, and everyone seemed to be having a great time. Then someone's loud scream shattered the joyous occasion.

"Guuuuun," someone screamed.

Two black teenagers stood behind where the DeMarcos were sitting, and they opened fire with automatic weapons. Ian covered his son and hit the floor. He crawled, with Christian under one arm, toward his daughter. He was forced to stop when a bullet hit him in his leg, burning his flesh as it pierced his calf muscle. Everything happened in less than ten seconds, but it seemed as if it took forever for the shots to stop flying. Once they did, his family would never be the same.

Colin, who was still holding little Brianna, was covered in blood. He was barely hanging on to his life, but he was the least of Ian's worries. He couldn't take his eyes off of his wife, Tasha, who was lying on her stomach with her head resting on the dirty floor, faceup, eyes still open yet motionless.

The men who worked for Colin returned fire, and the two attackers were on the floor, bleeding from the many bullet holes that riddled their young bodies. Ian crawled over to his wife, but she was gone. He looked up at his father and noticed that his daughter wasn't crying. She wasn't moving either. He left the crying Christian on the floor beside his now-deceased mother and jumped up and ran to his daughter. He grabbed his little girl from his father's arms and held her close to his heart. He was rocking her back and forth but couldn't bring himself to say anything.

"Brianna," he screamed, finally finding his voice. "Brianna baby, it's Daddy. Talk to me, baby. God," Ian screamed as he stared up at the ceiling. "Don't you do this to me! Briannnnnnnnaa. Brianna baby." His words were cut short by his tears. He heard his son crying, and he turned and ran to him. He sat down on the floor and held Brianna in one hand and checked his son's body for blood with the other.

Andrea ran over and picked up Christian. "I got him," she said as she cried. "Check on Brianna."

Ian turned his attention back to his daughter. He felt her neck to see if he could find a pulse, but she was already gone. It was the worst feeling in the world. He wished he could trade places with his daughter as he held her lifeless body in his arms. He felt helpless knowing that there was nothing he could do the save the love of his life. He sat on the floor beside his wife, holding his dead daughter, and couldn't believe what had just happened.

"Call an ambulance," somebody yelled. "Somebody, please call an ambulance."

Ian reached up and closed his wife's eyes while his filled with tears. He turned his head toward one of the teenagers who had caused all the carnage and noticed that he was still alive. The boy was breathing hard and fighting to stay alive.

Ian sat his daughter down on a chair and jumped up. He walked over and grabbed the gun by the teenager's right foot. The boy looked up with pleading eyes as he opened his mouth, gasping for air. The young thug shook his head as if begging Ian not to finish him off. Ian wasn't the least bit swayed as he fired the final five rounds of the gun into the boy's skinny body, leaving him dead.

Once the gun was empty, he reared back and threw it at the other teen, who was lying upside down, already dead. The .40-caliber weapon hit the boy in his face. Ian ran over to him and started beating the boy's dead body. He punched and punched and punched, but there was no amount of punishment that was going to give him back what he lost.

Once the smoke cleared, seven people had been killed, nine shot. Ian lost his wife, his daughter, his mother, and the will to carry on. If it weren't for his son, he would've taken his own life.

Now after last night's brainless moment, he was teetering on losing his son, too.

Chapter 2

Zola opened her eyes and stared up at the water-stained ceiling. Confused, she took a deep breath as she tried to gather herself. Was she where she thought she was? This couldn't be. She had to be dreaming. She pinched herself and felt the sting. She shot up in the bed like a jack-in-the-box. Her ribs were killing her as she instinctively reached for them. They hurt even more when she touched them.

"What in the world is going on?" she said, looking around at the familiar surroundings. Was this really real? She was hoping this was some horrible nightmare, but it wasn't.

Why was she here?

What happened?

How did she get here?

And of all the places in the world, why here?

Zola looked around the raggedy and run-down room and felt her heart start to race. She felt as if she was about to have a panic attack. She closed her eyes and tried to calm herself by taking slow and deliberate breaths. And her head! *My God*. It was aching something awful. She used both hands to massage her temples, hoping that would ease the pain, but lifting her arms up only hurt her ribs more.

Yet she couldn't even think about the pain because her mind was on this space she was in. There was something about where she was that caused her a great deal of discomfort. She tried to stop the pain between her ears by closing her eyes, but that didn't help. A tear made its way down the side of her face, but she quickly wiped it away.

She couldn't cry, wouldn't cry. Her life had never allowed much room for self-pity or weakness, but now was a time she wanted to let go. Death couldn't be this unpleasant, she thought. The tears she tried to stop paid her no mind and continued to flow. She closed her eyes again, but the stream of liquid pain kept flowing. And the fact that she couldn't stop crying made her want to cry even more.

She kept looking around the room, hoping the dirty walls would magically turn into the crisp and clean walls of her own home, but the more she stared, the dirtier the walls became.

How did I get here? she wondered again.

She racked her brain trying to come up with something, but she couldn't. The last thing she remembered was cooking dinner in her kitchen.

How did I get here? she thought over and over until she was mentally exhausted, yet nothing registered. Could she have been here all along and the beautiful home that cost a few hundred thousand dollars in the trendy Little Five Points area have been just a dream? What about the brand-new convertible Jaguar? Was that just a dream too? Could it all have been a fantasy? No, it couldn't have been, because if it was, her life was a total failure. She had been failed as a child, failed as a teenager, and now as an adult. The anxiety kicked in again, and her breathing became hard and heavy.

Zola forced herself to calm down and stared at the hideous-looking wall again. Her aching head got the better of her, and she was forced to lie back down. Something smelled bad. She reached underneath her head and removed the disgustingly greasy and stinking pillow that had long ago lost all its fluff. She frowned at the flat and nasty-looking thing and tossed it on the floor. She wanted to cry as the realization of where she was sank in. There were so many horrible memories in this room. She told herself that she would never enter this place again, and yet here she was looking at those same pathetic walls. She wanted to jump up and snatch that ugly wallpaper off those ugly walls and burn it, but she couldn't move. She was freezing cold, and the single-pane window wasn't doing much to stop the outside wind from coming into the room. The curtain flailed, letting her know that the old broken glass had never been fixed. She pulled the covers closer to her and tried not to cry.

Just yesterday she was living in heaven, and now she found herself back in hell. Zola kept searching her brain for any sign of what happened to her but kept coming up blank. After a few minutes of trying to retrace the last twenty-four hours, she stopped. She chuckled at how cruel life had been to her, and it all started in the very room she lay in. She had gone to sleep in a bed that cost almost $10,000, yet she woke up in one that reeked of urine, marijuana, and sex. She was in the same bed where she was raped. The rape was supposed to be a gift for her thirteenth birthday. What in the world did she ever do to anybody to deserve what life was throwing at her?

Zola stayed on her back for a full thirty minutes, saying and doing nothing. The radio alarm clock clicked to life, and Mary J. Blige crooned. Zola loved Mary. Well, old Mary. She couldn't relate to the new and happy Mary. But old Mary—beat-up Mary, frustrated Mary, broken Mary—yeah, that was her girl. The old Mary was her kin. They shared the same spirit. The pain and anguish in every word belted from the soul sister's tortured diaphragm spoke directly to her. There wasn't a song that old Mary ever created that didn't speak to and of Zola's trials and tribulations in this world as a young black woman.

It was time to pull herself up and figure out what was going on in her world. And the first thing she had to figure out was how she got back in this pissy-smelling bed. And where was her evil mother? Yet old Mary had her paralyzed by the rhythm. The bedroom door flew open, and there she was.

"Get yo' ass up, Zola," Sara, Zola's wicked mother, said as the door hit the wall so hard it bounced back toward her, forcing her to open it again. "This ain't no hotel. Now you let me lay down some ground rules right off the bat. Yo' ass ain't a child no more, so when I leave to go to work, you leave too. I'ma give you today to rest up since that fool you call a man done went upside your dumbass head. But make no mistake about it, tomorrow you better get to moving. Yo' brother is coming home today, and I promised the parole board that he had a place to stay. And he's staying in here, so don't get comfortable."

Sara gave Zola one last pathetic look as if she had smelled some sour milk, then turned on her heels and slammed the door behind her.

"Well, good morning to you too, Mother dear," Zola said as she sat up on the side of the bed. She ran her tongue across her lip, and an instant pain shot through her body. She touched it and felt something dried and flaky on the side of her face. It had to be blood. Zola's mind raced again as to what had happened to her, but she couldn't remember anything.

This was crazy.

She looked around and found her purse sitting on the raggedy plaid tweed love seat, which sat in the corner of the filthy room. She grabbed her purse and looked inside for her mobile phone. The screen of her BlackBerry said she had seven missed calls, all from Andre. She hit the little green telephone icon and called his phone. The phone rang four times, then went to his voicemail, but she didn't leave a message. She ended the call and hit the redial but still didn't get an answer. While she was waiting for that long-winded woman Sprint hired to prompt the caller, she opened her purse and noticed that all her money was missing. Either she had completely lost her mind or Sara had robbed her. Perhaps it was both.

"Hey. Where are you? Give me a call. I'm at my mom's house, and I . . . Anyway, call me when you get this message."

Zola reached over toward the nightstand and turned the radio off. She sat there thinking, still racking her mind to find some answers to what landed her back in this hellhole of a house. And what happened to her face? She wanted to scream, but what good was that going to do? She couldn't think of one single time in her twenty-seven years on this earth when she was truly happy. She stood and felt so unstable that she almost fell back down onto the bed, but she used her hand to break the fall.

Zola shook her head to help clear it and tried it again. This time she found some equilibrium and moved slowly until she felt stable enough to move quickly. She held on to the walls as she walked out of the bedroom and across the hallway into the bathroom. Once in the bathroom, she pulled the string hanging from the light switch. It was as if someone had lit a candle, but the room remained dimly lit. Zola was happy for the lack of light because what she saw staring back at her from the reflection in the broken mirror frightened her.

Oh, my God!

Her face almost scared her to death. Both of her eyes were severely darkened and bloodshot, her dark chocolate–colored cheeks were now almost purple, and her lip appeared to be beyond the need for stitches.

"What in the hell has happened to me?" she said.

She couldn't believe what she was seeing. Then her eyes roamed her face to the nasty gash on her forehead. It was an old scar that had somehow reopened. The original scar was given to her by a drunken Sara, who would sometimes attack her for no reason. Who had reopened it was a big mystery.

Zola stared at herself. Dark skin, straight and wavy hair, high cheekbones, eyes larger than normal yet slanted. Every time she looked in the mirror, she wondered what her true heritage was. She looked different, always did. She was always called ugly because nobody could identify with her. She was black but mixed with something else.

Who was her daddy?

Where was he?

Did he even know she existed?

Whenever she asked Sara about her daddy, the only response she ever received was, "Why the hell you keep asking me that? Don't I take care of you good enough? Don't worry about who ya daddy is. He ain't worrying about you."

Zola turned on the water and waited for it to warm up. She placed a dab of toothpaste on the tip of her finger and brushed her teeth. The paste hurt her lip, so she stopped. She bent down and rinsed her mouth out. She needed to see a doctor and wondered why she wasn't in the hospital instead of this hellhole of a house. Everything was hurting. She grabbed a hard and well-used hand towel. She ran the hot water and soap over it until it was clean enough to wash her face. She looked back into the mirror and ran her hand along the scar that had been with her for most of her life.

Zola's mind went back to the day when she was 9 years old and somehow found the audacity to pour out her mother's liquor. She hated seeing that ugly green bottle of Tanqueray. Whenever that bottle was around, her mother turned into a very evil person. When Sara wasn't drinking the stuff in that green bottle, she was the perfect mother who laughed and helped her kids do their homework. She even sat at the kitchen table and played board games with Zola and all the neighborhood kids. But once the green bottle came into play, she quickly became Satan's favorite child.

On Zola's thirteenth birthday, Sara was sipping the contents of that green bottle pretty hard. She started drinking early in the morning, and Zola couldn't help but wish her birthday was on a school day. Sara had said she was celebrating her daughter becoming a woman.

"Five more years and your ass is gone," Sara said when Zola walked into the kitchen to get her morning glass of orange juice and a muffin. "But happy birthday anyway with ya ugly self."

Zola didn't speak to her mother when she was drinking, so she poured herself glass of orange juice and ignored the drunken woman.

"I know you wondering what I got you for your li'l birthday, but it's a surprise. I'll give it to you tonight," she said. "Well, I won't give it to you, but . . ." Sara slurred in her drunken state. "You'll be happy. Put it that way."

Zola walked out of the kitchen and out of the house. She spent the entire day at her friend's house hoping that Sara would be asleep when she returned.

No such luck.

When Zola returned, she went straight to her bedroom and closed the door. She turned on her music to try to drown out the aggravating sound of her mother's voice.

"'Happy birthday to you,'" Sara sang in her drunken haze. "'Happy birthday to youuuu, Zola. Happy birthday to you.'"

Zola lay on her bed, hoping that her mother would shut up, but then her bedroom door opened. She looked up to see Sara and Richard. Richard was Sara's ugly boyfriend who nobody liked. At that moment, he wasn't wearing anything but his boxer underwear.

"Tonight is the night," Sara sang as if she were Betty Wright, "Richard makes you a woman."

Richard walked into the room and stood over her. Zola hated the sight of this man. He was black as tar and had the most rotten teeth she'd ever seen. His beard was nappy, the hair on his head was nappy, and even his chest hair was nappy. It looked like some burned taco meat. He started dancing a slow dance as if he was trying to turn her on. He slid his hands in his underwear and smiled. "You ready?" he asked.

"You better get your ugly self away from me. Get out of my room," Zola yelled.

"Oh," Richard said as he moved closer to her. "Sara, we got us a fighter on our hands."

"She bet' not fight," Sara said. "Get her ass tore up in here."

Zola was scared out of her mind of what the nasty man had in store for her, but she feared her mother even more. Sara's words paralyzed her.

Richard sat on the side of her bed and put his hand on her leg. She jumped and started to cry.

"Don't cry, baby girl. This gon' feel good," he said. "Big Rick knows how to please a woman. And since you thirteen, that makes you a woman."

"You got to make her a woman," Sara said.

Zola protested and threatened to tell.

Sara reached back and slapped her so hard she saw stars. She didn't fight anymore. She lay on the bed and allowed the pedophile to have his way.

Zola would forever be haunted by her mother's laughter while the man forced his grown penis all the way inside of her virgin vagina.

"Ha-ha-haaaaa," Sara laughed. "Oh, hush your faking. I know you been running your li'l fast ass around here with them boys."

"Noooo," Zola cried, trying desperately to make eye contact with her mother to plead with her to put an end to this madness, but there would be no help coming.

"Listen, bitch," Sara said, "you shut all that damn whining up right now. I'm doing you a favor. You know how many girls would love for they momma to let them have sex? You ain't got a pretty bone in your body, so ain't nobody gonna wanna fuck you. You should be happy you got a momma who will hook you up. Now shut your ugly ass up and enjoy your birthday present."

"Momma, please make him stop," Zola cried, but all she got was her mother fanning her off and leaving the room. She left her alone with the evil man who was on top of her, pushing and grunting as if he had lost his mind.

Zola went limp. She stopped fighting, she stopped crying, and she just lay completely still while her mother's boyfriend carried out his perverted desires with her innocent body. Once the rape was done, the man rolled over and lay on his back, trying to catch his breath.

"Aww, that was good," he said. "You okay?"

Zola was momentarily paralyzed. What had just happened? Her mind couldn't process it in full. She just knew that she had been violated in the worst way.

Zola calmly stood up and walked over to the raggedy love seat in the corner of her bedroom and picked up her book bag. She unzipped the pocket where she kept her writing utensils and removed a black ballpoint pen. She didn't think. She just acted.

Richard still lay in the same spot, smiling to himself. He kept that look of euphoria until Zola jumped on top of him and aimed her pen straight for his neck. She could feel the plastic pierce his skin and the muscle.

Richard jumped up and stumbled into the wall, holding his neck while blood shot out of his wound like a faucet turned on high. He was screaming in pain, but Zola was relentless. She stalked him, stabbing wherever she could reach. She punctured the skin on his back, arms, and stomach with the pointy pen, determined to return some of the pain he'd caused her. Richard's eyes bulged as he was stabbed over and over by the little girl who had just brought him so much pleasure. Yet he screamed now as she gave him pain like he had never experienced in his life.

A noise from the door caught Zola's attention as she realized that Sara had run into the room when she heard all the commotion. Seeing her mother caused Zola to turn her attention and anger toward her. She stopped stabbing Richard and went after Sara with the bloody pen.

Sara screamed, turned, and ran from the house as if she were a track star. But Zola chased her, catching her twice in the back with the pen before Zola tripped over a tree stump and fell. She looked up to see her mother holding her shoulder and crying for someone to call the cops.

The police showed up, and Sara told a lie that truly bothered Zola. She told the police that she had come home to find her man and her daughter having sex. She said she confronted them, and Zola started stabbing the man, saying he was raping her. And then the girl flipped out and started attacking her, too. The rape had Zola in shock, and she was unable to even tell her side of the story.

Zola was removed from the house and taken directly to a juvenile detention center where she was charged with attempted murder. Luckily for Zola, Richard didn't die from his multiple stab wounds and was too scared to testify on his own behalf. No one ever saw Richard after that.

Richard was gone, but Zola's memories remained and took a heavy toll on her. That day had changed everything. Before the rape, Zola was a normal kid. She got great grades and participated in everything her middle school had to offer. Her favorite sport was softball, and she was the starting pitcher for her school's team, but the fact that that man had forced himself on her with the blessings of her mother, and the subsequent lie Sara told the authorities, killed her spirit. She became depressed and withdrawn. She rarely smiled and never played sports again.

While Zola was sitting in a juvenile detention center waiting for her day in court, she was paid a visit by her middle school math teacher, Dr. Carolyn Rogers. Dr. Rogers was a lovely woman who had an affinity with any child born into poverty. She always had a way of getting Zola to open up to her, especially when things weren't the greatest at home.

Zola never wanted to talk about her thirteenth birthday gift from her mother, but as usual, Dr. Rogers figured out a way to get it out of her. She told her everything, and less than forty-eight hours after their conversation, the cops rushed in and arrested Sara for cruelty to children, sexual assault, and a host of other crimes. After all the evidence was presented, it was Sara who ended up in jail instead of Zola. She took a plea deal that sent her to the Georgia Penitentiary for Women on a sentence of nine and a half years. She got out on good behavior after five years. A warrant was also issued for

Richard's arrest, and he was placed on Georgia's most wanted list, but the last Zola checked, he was still on the run.

Zola was released from the juvenile detention center and allowed to live with her grandparents, who already had custody of Zola's younger brother, Ravon. Momma Mary and Daddy James were already in their late seventies and not really in any condition to care for two energetic teenagers. Knowing they didn't have much adult supervision, Zola and Ravon ran wild. After the rape, Zola swore she would never have sex again, but somehow the exact opposite happened. She started using her body to get what she wanted from men. Money was always tight in the Jameses' household because her grandparents were on a fixed income. The little extra they received from the State for taking custody of two children barely fed Ravon.

Teenagers can be cruel, and if you add poverty and low self-esteem to the mix, they can be downright brutal. If there was one good thing about Sara, she kept them wearing nice clothes, but that luxury went away when they went to live with Momma Mary and Daddy James. Goodwill clothes and hand-me-downs were all they would get. This transition was especially hard on Zola. She was already considered the ugly duckling. The only redeeming quality she had was her sense of fashion, but with Sara in prison, that lone plus was now a minus.

That superficial and materialistic slight led her to running around with the neighborhood hustlers. The guys who were making fast money bought her the clothes she wanted, and she gave them the sex they said they needed. This simple yet devastating decision led her down a long and treacherous path of one bad man after another. When she turned 17, she stepped up her game. She was tired of the boys and started dating older men. She thought she had found the right man who would stop the vicious cycle, but she had a rude awakening when she realized she was pregnant. The dreams she had of them living happily ever after went flying out the window once she had the baby. She showed up at her baby daddy's office, which just happened to belong to the principal of her high school, and asked for assistance. She was scolded by the man, called everything except the child of God, and told to stay away from him. Once again, she confided in Dr. Rogers, the same woman who helped put Sara away, and sure enough the principal was brought to justice as well. But unlike Sara, the principal wasn't going to be paraded across the news as a child molester. Realizing his career was over, he placed the barrel of a .357 Magnum in his mouth and ended it all right there in his office. Rumors ran rampant, and Zola was forced to leave school. She never went back.

Zola rubbed the scar again as her past came crashing down on her. Then, all of a sudden, she looked around the small and run-down room and realized that she had to leave. She pulled the string to turn the light off and left the room. She walked back into the bedroom where she had slept and gathered her things. All she had were her purse, the clothes on her back, and a cashmere coat, which was hanging over the arm of the love seat. She walked back out into the living room where Sara was sitting on the same raggedy sofa they had as kids. She was smoking a cigarette and watching an episode of some reality show on television.

Zola stood in the doorway staring at the woman who had tried her best to ruin her life. Sara seemed old and beaten up. Her once pretty and flawless caramel skin was now filled with pockmarks, dark spots, and wrinkles. Her eyes were lifeless, and her once long and silky hair was now a gray bird nest of a mess. It had been at least three, maybe four, years since Zola had last seen her mother, and had she not found herself here now, forever could've passed and she wouldn't have cared. Their past would never allow them to share that sacred mother-and-daughter bond.

"How did I get here?" Zola asked.

Sara never looked away from her show. She laughed at something one of the actors said and acted as if Zola didn't exist.

"Well, can you tell me what happened to the money that was in my purse?"

Sara turned the volume down with the remote and turned to her daughter. "I want you to know one thing," Sara said with as much venom as she could muster. "I don't owe you nothing. I paid my price for whatever transgression you think I made against you. So as far as I'm concerned, we are even. You rang my doorbell, and I let you in. Whatever money you had in your purse when you got here should still be there." With that, she turned back to the television and turned the volume up high.

"How did I get here? Who brought me here?"

"I don't know, Zola. I turned on the light, and you were on the porch sitting in the chair. I saw a white truck, one of those SUV things, pulling off, and that's all I can tell you. Now if you don't mind, I'd like to get back to my damn show."

"Why are you such a bitch? What have I ever done to you?"

"What have you ever done to me? How dare you ask me that? I went to prison because of your ass."

"You went to prison because you allowed your thirteen-year-old daughter to be raped by an old-ass man. The courts found that to be a fucking crime, and so did I."

"Just leave me the hell alone," Sara said as she turned back toward the television.

"I wish it had been you I stabbed in the neck. And I wish you had died a very slow and painful death," Zola said. "I couldn't hate you any more if I tried. You are the most despicable woman I've ever met."

"Thank you," Sara said. "Now get the hell out of my house."

Zola had to hold herself back from attacking the woman who had given her life. She looked at her mother and shook her head. She was beyond pitiful, and all of a sudden, for the first time in her life, Zola felt sorry for her. Obviously, she had some serious and deep-rooted issues that made her act this way.

Zola walked over to her mother and looked down at her. The two women stared into each other's eyes: Sara looking up from her sitting spot on the sofa, and Zola looking down on her as the child had become the mother. Neither one of them said a word until Zola smiled, shook her head, and turned on her heels. She walked over to the door, looked back at her mother who was now sitting with her head down in shame, and walked out of the house. She had no idea where she was headed or how she was going to get there, but she had to leave.

Chapter 3

Ian drove onto his street, which was off of Ralph David Abernathy Boulevard in Atlanta's historic West End, and took in his surroundings. He looked to his left and saw Harry and Willie, two old guys whose best days were far behind them. Life had beaten them down so much that they seemed to have quit living. They were sitting on the curb beside each other. Willie was a Vietnam War veteran who always wore a long sword in a sleeve connected to his belt. He was talking his raggedy mouth off while his friend Harry stared off in the distance, ignoring his drinking buddy. Willie handed a brown paper bag to Harry, and that got the attention of his hard-faced friend. Standing behind them were a couple of younger guys wearing big coats and looking very much like the low-level drug dealers they were. Across the street from the thugs and the winos were a few crack addicts who were trying desperately to sell their sickly-looking bodies to whoever could afford $10 or $15. Ian waved at Trudy, a woman he found to be very interesting. She was once a well-respected pediatrician who had her own office complex in Virginia, but looking at her now, you would never believe that she ever finished high school.

Ian turned into the driveway of his ranch-style bungalow. His house needed a paint job and some work done on the gutters, but otherwise it was in pretty good shape. He did a double take and noticed a big black Lincoln Town Car idling on the curb across the street from his house. He had a visitor. His nerves kicked into overdrive.

Is this it?

Were they coming for him?

Ian took his eyes off the car and trained them on the man standing on his porch.

"Ian," Trudy said, rushing up to his driver's side, "I need a big favor. I got this little problem and . . . Hey, baby," she said, waving at Christian and trying to buy a little time so she could come up with a good lie.

Ian held up a hand and never took his eyes off the man. He removed his wallet from his rear pocket and grabbed a $5 bill. He handed the money to Trudy, but she didn't take off like she normally did. She stood there staring at the visitor just as he did.

A tall, well-dressed man stood on the porch with his hands in his pockets. He wore a suit that fit so nicely it had to be custom-made. The man adjusted his black cashmere topcoat, wrapped his stylish scarf a little closer to his neck, and stepped down from the porch. A slick black felt fedora was his crown, and he tapped it in Trudy's direction.

"Hey," Trudy said as if the man's eyes held some hypnotic potion. "How you doing?"

"Good morning. How are you?" the man said with an easy smile.

"I'd be better if I had a few dollars to get me something to eat," Trudy said, rubbing her stomach for effect.

The man smiled and reached into his breast pocket. He pulled out an eel-skin wallet, opened it, and removed a $50 bill. "Well, today is your lucky day. Have a meal on me."

"Thank you," Trudy said as she quickly snatched the money from the man's well-manicured hands. "You're a very kind man. God will bless you abundantly, and may all your—"

"No problem. Have a good day," he said, cutting her off in midsentence. There was no mistaking that he really meant for her to get the hell on about her business.

"You a'ight, Ian?" Trudy asked before she moved, though she was clearly twitching to be on her way.

Ian nodded, and Trudy walked off, looking back at the man with a very suspicious eye.

Ian's fear of the authorities dissipated and was replaced by something even deeper. He was experiencing an emotion that he'd spent the last three years trying to put a finger on. To the naked eye, everything about this man said power and respect, but to him, the mere sight of him meant pain and anguish. Ian turned his vehicle off and stared at the man who looked just like him. With the exception of a few wrinkles under the eyes and on the forehead, and a little salt-and-pepper hair peeking out from underneath the feathered brim, they could pass for twins.

Colin DeMarco walked toward Ian's driver side door, then noticed something. He stopped, shifted his course, and a wide smile appeared on his normally stoic face as he picked up his pace and headed to the passenger's side. He looked in the back window and almost snatched the door off its hinges to get to the smiling little boy in the back seat.

Christian stared at the man with a hint of familiarity. Then it was as if something registered, telling him that this was the man who always gave him lots of gifts.

Colin DeMarco stood in the doorway of his son's 10-year-old Ford Explorer and lifted his grandson from the seat. He gave him a quick kiss on the cheek, then pushed him high into the air, then brought him back down for a tight embrace. "Oh, my goodness, look how big you've gotten. Geez, I'm going to have to stop letting so much time go by without seeing you. What's it been?"

Colin said, shooting Ian a nasty look. "Six, maybe seven months. That's just shameful."

"You wanna see my car? It's my favorite," Christian said with wide, big brown eyes.

"Let me see what you got," Colin said.

"It's fast, too," Christian said as he twisted for his grandfather to let him down. Once he was on the ground, he jumped back into the car and retrieved his prized possession. Christian held up a yellow Corvette, which had seen better days. The paint was chipped, and one of the tires was missing. "I broke the tire, but my dad said he's gonna fix it."

Colin reached out and grabbed his grandson's toy and studied the replica. He nodded. "Sporty yet classy. I like it. Guess what Granddaddy has for you," Colin said.

"What?"

"I'll be right back," Colin said as he walked over to the porch. "Close your eyes," he said with his hands behind his back as he returned. "Now open them."

Colin smiled as he handed his grandson a shiny black model Lamborghini.

"Oh, yeah. Wow," Christian said, smiling from ear to ear. He threw his tattered Corvette on the ground and stood in awe of his new ride. "Thank you. Hey, Daddy, look at what Granddaddy got me. This is cool."

"That's nice," Ian said as he walked around the truck to where his son and father were standing. He couldn't hide the fact that his feelings were a little hurt by the tossing of what used to be his son's favorite car. He walked over and picked up the old car and wiped it off.

"Only the best for my grandson," Colin said, smiling from ear to ear. He read the look on his son's face. "Relax, Ian, it's only a toy."

"So what brings you over here?" Ian asked, cutting to the chase.

"What kind of question is that?" Colin snapped. "I have a son and a grandson standing in front of me. That's what brings me over here. Maybe if you made your way out to see me sometime, I wouldn't have to show up unannounced," Colin said. "Now act like you were raised with some sense and invite me in."

No matter how much he wanted to hate his father, he didn't and he couldn't. His father was a very good man to those he cared for. He was a family man to the core, but the line of work he chose wrecked Ian's own family. And that was something he would never forget or forgive his father for.

Ian rubbed his son's head, and they walked toward his house. Once inside Ian's small yet tidy home, Christian took off running over the hardwood floors to his bedroom. He returned before the two men could get into any meaningful conversation with each other. He had an armful of model cars to show his grandfather.

"Well, look what we have here," Colin said in amazement. "Man, you're a serious collector. Which one is your favorite?"

Christian held up the new Lamborghini, then looked around for his old Corvette. "Daddy, can I go outside and get my car? I must've dropped it."

"Here," Ian said, handing him the car with only three wheels.

"Hey," Christian said, reaching out for the old car. "What are you doing with my car, Daddy?"

"You threw it on the ground," Ian said as he rubbed his son's bushy hair.

"So those two are your favorites, huh? I like that. Always be loyal. New stuff is cool, but old stuff has meaning. Always remember that, Christian."

"Thank you."

"Have a seat," Ian said as he fiddled around nervously in the kitchen. His dad showing up was not a social call. That much he knew for sure.

Colin looked around and picked a chair facing the door. Even though Christian didn't spend much time with his grandfather, seeing him maybe three or four times a year, he acted like they were the best of friends. He jumped into the old man's lap and ran his cars on an imaginary racing track in the air. It was amazing what a new toy could do for a child.

Colin ate it up as he smiled and hugged his grandson.

"Christian," Ian said, "it's nap time, buddy."

"But I'm not sleepy. I wanna stay with Granddaddy for a little while," he protested.

"Son," Ian said in a stern voice, "what did I say?"

"Hey, big guy, listen," Colin said. "Let me see those muscles."

Christian frowned but flexed his little arm anyway.

"What the . . . Man, you're strong. But if you want those things to keep getting bigger, you gotta get your rest. Give me twenty push-ups," Colin said as he lifted his grandson up and placed him on the floor. "One, two, three . . ." Colin said, holding in his laughter at the funniest push-ups he'd ever seen. "Boy, look at him go. Sixteen, seventeen, eighteen, nineteen, twenty."

"I'm tired," Christian said, breathing hard and rubbing his arms.

"Well, give me a big hug, and go do what your daddy asked you to do," Colin said as he reached out for a long embrace with his grandson. He kissed him on the forehead and savored the moment.

"Okay," Christian said.

"I know I don't get to see you that much, but I want you to know that your granddaddy loves you very much, okay?"

"Okay," Christian said. "See you later, Granddaddy."

"Later, alligator," Colin said.

Once Christian was off to his room, Ian walked back into the living room. "Can I get you something to drink?"

"No, thank you," Colin said, turning to his son. His smile was now replaced by a serious glare. "I wanna know what happened last night. And I don't need you to leave out any details."

Chapter 4

Zola walked down Metropolitan Boulevard toward the MARTA bus station. Cars blew their horns in hopes that she was a prostitute working the strip, but she ignored them and continued on her way. She didn't have one dollar to her name and had no idea how she was going to get back to her house, but she had to get moving. Sara's house wasn't an option. Not that she was welcome there in the first place, but even if she were, there were too many bad memories between those walls for her to even consider it. Yet there was a small part of her that wanted Sara to call out to her and ask her to come back. Maybe she could say she was sorry about everything that she ever allowed to happen and ask for forgiveness. Zola even found herself looking back toward her childhood house as she walked away, but she knew it was in vain. The woman who had given her life was physically and mentally incapable of showing any trace of motherly love.

Zola made it to the corner of Metropolitan and Eastside Avenue and sat down on the MARTA bench. The wind slapped her across her face, and she felt the cuts and bruises scream in pain, but she endured. She reached into her purse and removed an oversized pair of sunglasses and put them on. Maybe they would stop people from staring at her blackened eyes.

A bus pulled up, people got on and people got off, but she remained seated. The driver motioned with his hands as if asking her what she was going to do, but she ignored him. He closed the door and pulled off. Zola opened her purse and removed her cell phone. She dialed Andre's number again and was sent to the voicemail.

"Hey, this is me. Where are you? Call me," she said, then hit the END button on her BlackBerry.

A crazy-looking woman was standing across the street at the gas station. She wore a purple church hat, a white full-length coat, and a pair of cowboy boots. She was screaming at the top of her lungs, "All of you sinners, God has spoken to me and told me that Jesus is coming back soon. All sinners better repent or face the wrath. Eternal damnation is the price you'll pay." She repeated it over and over. "All of you sinners. God has spoken to me and told me that Jesus is coming back soon. All sinners better repent or face the wrath. Eternal damnation is the price you'll pay. All of you sinners . . ."

Zola stared at the woman and wondered if her chaotic message was meant for her. She didn't believe in coincidence. In her world, everything and everybody happened for a reason. The woman was screaming so loud that she almost lost her voice.

Zola had not so much as picked up a Bible in her entire life. Momma Mary and Daddy James used to take her to church when she was small, but after a while they stopped showing up at Sara's house to pick her up, and when she lived with them, they didn't even bother to wake her or Ravon up for their Sunday services. And Sara was such a devil she never even mentioned the word "church," so Zola and her brother never went. Yet she couldn't block the woman's voice from her head.

"You are a sinner," the woman yelled as she pointed at Zola.

Zola looked around to see who the crazy head case was talking to. She didn't see anyone, so she turned back around and looked at the woman, who was still pointing at her. She pulled her shades down over her nose and peered at the woman.

The woman stopped screaming and leaned forward to get a clear look at Zola. Her eyes grew wide to the size of silver dollars, and she covered her mouth as if she was trying to stifle a scream. She pointed to the heavens and then back at Zola.

"The devil is here," she screamed as if Zola were sitting on the bench with horns, hooves, and a long tail. The woman backed up, then turned on her heels and took off running down the street, her long coat flowing behind her like a cape.

"Crazy bitch," Zola said to herself.

She sat there for a few minutes taking in the scene of people living their lives in the ghetto. She tried to block it out, but the crazy lady's words kept coming back to her. There was something there, but she couldn't put her finger on it. She wrapped her arms around herself and rocked slowly. What was she going to do? She felt alone and afraid. The last time she felt this way she was sitting alone in a cold jail cell for attempted murder.

Zola closed her eyes, and for the first time in her life, she asked God to help her. She had never been a very religious nor spiritual woman and wasn't even sure how to pray. But something deep inside of her was telling her that if there were ever a time to try this God thing, it was now. She was beaten, broken, and all alone. She closed her eyes as tight as she could and just started talking to God. She prayed as hard as she could, halfway expecting God to fix her life right then and there. When she opened her eyes, she saw an angel.

"What the hell?" Ravon, her brother, fresh out of prison, said with a wide smile.

Ravon stood before her, showing all thirty-two of the cleanest, whitest teeth she had ever seen. He wore a pair of crisp Levi jeans and a black hooded sweatshirt, which was underneath a big goose down coat, and a brand-new pair of Timberland work boots. A big gold chain with a medallion of the crucifixion of Christ hung from his neck.

Zola removed her shades to make sure she wasn't seeing things. "Oh, my God," she said as she jumped up to hug the one person who always had her back.

"Whatchu doing out here sleeping?"

"I'm not asleep, boy. I was praying," Zola said as she held her brother in a long embrace. It had been five years since she had been able to touch him. She visited him about three or four times a year, and it was always behind thick three-inch prison glass.

"Praying?" Ravon said. "Now that's good to know. The last time I talked to you I asked you to start reading your Bible, and you said you would pass."

"Did you see me reading a Bible, or did you see me praying?"

"I see you still a smart-ass. You look like crap. What happened to you?"

"When did you get out?" Zola asked, ignoring his question.

"Last night. Well, really about three in the morning. I'm so happy to be out of that place I don't know what to do," Ravon said as he shook his head at the memories of a place he hoped to never see again. "It almost feels like a dream. If it is, I hope I don't wake up back in that hellhole."

"Well, try to stay out this time for more than a month or two. You've been in and out of jail since you were twelve years old, Ravon. Don't you think it's time for something different?"

"Yeah. And I promise you that I'm done with that life. Gotta leave it behind me. I'm a grown man now. Got my girl Lisa. She's been riding with me the whole bid,"

Ravon said, smiling. "That's my baby. Gon' get married and everything."

"Oh, Lord," Zola said.

"What happened to your face, Zola?" Ravon said. His smile was replaced by a menacing snarl. "And eye?"

"I don't know," Zola said, putting her shades back on. "I need to get home."

"Whatchu mean you don't know? That busta beat you up?"

"I don't know what happened. I woke up at Sara's house, and I don't even know how I got there."

Ravon studied his sister without responding. "So where are you headed, Zo?"

"Home."

"Where is home?"

"Little Five Points."

"Little Five Points? What you doing living over there?'

"Living. Which is better than what I was doing over here." Zola swept her hand around the ghetto that surrounded her, then bent over in pain. "My side is killing me."

"Have you seen a doctor?"

"No."

"Well, that's where we are going," Ravon said as he walked his sister over to the gold Honda Accord parked on the corner.

"I'm all right."

"No, you're not," Ravon said.

"Whose car is this?"

"Lisa's. I'm supposed to be meeting this dude about a job."

"You're not wasting any time, huh?"

"Can't. I've wasted fourteen years of my time in and out of that damn penitentiary. I gotta get a job," Ravon said. "I'm tired of this street crap. Going legit, Zo."

"I'll believe that when I see it," Zola said. "I wish I had a dollar for every time I've heard that one."

"Well, keep your eyes open, big sis."

"How did you know where I was?" Zola asked as she buckled her seat belt.

"I went by Sara's, but before I could get out of the car, old, nosy Ms. Ham from next door told me she saw you. She's still crazy as hell. She was standing out on the porch looking a hot damn mess. Had on a bra and a thong, trying to seduce me with those old, bony-ass legs," Ravon said, shaking his head. "That chick is crazier than Sara."

"Mrs. Ham was out there? I didn't see her when I left."

"She came running out, trying to hug me. The woman is nothing but skin and bones. I asked where her clothes were, and she had the audacity to tell me to come in the house with her and she'd take the rest of them off. Caked-on makeup, bright orange lipstick that missed all of her lips. Man, I turned around and got back in the car as fast as I could."

Zola shook her head as she pictured her old neighbor standing in the front yard in her unmentionables. Ms. Ham had always been a hot mess and would always tell anyone who would listen that she used to model for *Ebony*. She said her career was cut short because a fellow model got jealous and poured some scalding water on her, ruining her flawless face that paid her hundreds of thousands of dollars. Ms. Ham was almost six feet tall and was so skinny you could see her bones.

"Back to Sara. I called her to let her know I was on the way, and she was ranting and raving about you and how you never appreciated her. How she was a great mom. Not a good one, a great one. But I realize that Sara has some serious mental problems. You know she's crazy, right?"

"Yeah," Zola said, nodding her head. "Something is definitely wrong with her."

"I'm serious. You'd be surprised how many crazy-ass people are walking around this earth like they're regular. And all because nobody ever told them they were cuckoo."

"Speaking of crazy," Zola said, "you just missed this nut standing right across the street yelling at me. She kept calling me a sinner. But then when I looked at her, she took off running down the street. I'm talking about fast, too. Then she had the nerve to have on some damn cowboy boots."

Ravon jerked his head in the direction Zola was pointing. He smiled. "She scared you, huh? That's why you're out here praying."

"She didn't scare me, but I wasn't taking any chances. I'm just saying."

Ravon laughed. "Yeah, I hear ya. Anyway, old, freaky-ass Ms. Ham told me that she just saw you walking down the street, and here you are."

"Yeah, okay," Zola said with her joy showing all over her battered face. "I'm really happy to see you, Ray."

"I'm happy to see you too, big sis. And I know I've told you this a million times, but I'm sorry about what I did. My carelessness cost you more than I—"

"Ray," Zola said, holding up a hand to stop him from forcing her to relive a scene that took her years to get over. She still wasn't really over it. "Let's leave the past in the past."

Ravon looked at his sister and frowned. The more he looked at her, the more concern showed on his face. She had had such a rough go at life, and he couldn't bear the fact that he had added to that pain. The mere thought of what he did ate at him on a daily basis.

"Zo," he said, "you're the strongest woman I know. Since I've been gone, I've had lots of time to reflect, and

I know there aren't many people who could stand up to what you've been through, but I'm standing here looking at you. I'm not liking what I'm seeing. Now the one thing I could always count on was you coming out on top, but I don't know. What's going on?"

Zola stared off into the distance. She wasn't ready for this Ravon. She could tell right away that her brother wasn't the same guy he was five years ago. He was different—wiser and more mature. But she had been down this road before, and only time would tell with him.

Her mind wandered, and she couldn't help but wonder when or if she would ever find peace of mind. She could never seem to get into the groove of life because she was always fighting a new battle. But truth be told, she had been trying to figure out why her life was always in constant turmoil. What was it about her that made life want to kick her down a long flight of stairs? Losing her son was the hardest thing she had ever endured, and she thought about him and how he was snatched away from her. Her mind drifted back to that day.

It was a Friday evening, and Zola had been looking forward to this day for two weeks. She had a hot date with a man who had something going for himself. He was a police officer, single, no kids, tall, dark, and absolutely gorgeous. To make him even more appealing, he was heavily into volunteering with underprivileged children.

Zola asked Ravon if he could come over to her apartment and babysit her 3-year-old son, Jason. Something told her to call the date off when Ravon showed up looking like he had already smoked half a tree of marijuana, but she didn't want to lose out on this good man who seemed to be crazy about her. So against her better judgment, she made Ravon swear that he wouldn't let anything happen to her son and headed out for a night on the town with the first man who ever called her pretty.

Everything was going better than she had planned it. They were sitting at an upscale restaurant, enjoying a lovely view of ice skaters in Centennial Park. Her date talked about his dreams and aspirations as well as asked about hers. When she couldn't come up with anything, he forced her to think of something. He complimented her so much that it seemed as if he was trying too hard, but it still seemed genuine. They finished their meals and ordered dessert. He had a hot brownie with vanilla ice cream, and she had the red velvet cheesecake. Just as they were finishing up their last crumbs, her cell phone rang.

She ignored it the first time, hoping Ravon was just calling to check on her. Then it rang again. She knew there was a problem, but for the first time in her life she was having a great time with a man who never even mentioned sex. She ignored the second call. But then after the third call, she knew she had to get it. And something else told her that her perfect evening was about to come to a screeching halt. Oh, how she wanted to hold on to just a few more minutes of bliss. But the phone seemed to ring louder with each passing second. Was it the phone or was that her mother's intuition telling her that something was wrong with her child? She looked at the man sitting across from her and knew that he was too good to be true.

"Marvin," she said. "I need to take this."

"Go ahead," he said, ever the gentleman. "Take your time."

Zola excused herself, stood, and walked to the bathroom to take the call.

Ravon's frantic scream shook her to the core. Without even being able to make out the words he was babbling

*through his own tears, she knew something horrible
had happened to her son. She ran from the restroom
and rushed from the restaurant without even looking
Marvin's way. Luckily, he saw her. He jumped up,
reached in his wallet, and dropped three $50 bills on the
table before rushing after her.*

*"I need to get home. Something has happened to my
son."*

*Marvin waved the valet over and told him to hurry.
The car appeared in no time, he handed the young boy a
$5 bill, and he drove like a bat out of hell toward Zola's
spot in the hood. When they arrived, the ambulance was
already loading little Jason in the back. Zola thanked
Marvin and told him she would call him later. He
insisted on staying, but she wasn't hearing anything he
had to say, and she jumped out of his car and into the
back of the ambulance. She rode with her unconscious
son to Grady Memorial Hospital.*

*Ravon came in and met Zola, who was now waiting
in the emergency waiting room. He sat down beside her
and told her everything. He told her how they played
hide-and-go-seek, how they did push-ups, and about
all of the fun things they enjoyed doing until Jason was
worn out. Once the little guy fell asleep, Ravon admitted
that he got down to the business of bagging up his crack
cocaine for resale. He took a little break from his bagging to smoke a joint and watch a few rap videos. He
had been up for almost twenty-four hours straight, and
his body was shutting down. The weed didn't help his
sleep-deprived body, because before he knew it, he was
fast asleep.*

*At some point during the night, Jason woke up. He
stumbled upon the plastic bags of crack cocaine that
Ravon had carelessly left sitting on the coffee table, and
obviously thinking it was candy, he took a bite. A few*

minutes later, the little boy started crying and trying to spit. He yelled for his uncle to wake up.

"Candy nasty," he said as his little face frowned in pain. "Candy nasty, Uncle Wayvon."

Ravon looked around and noticed that half of his drugs were tossed on the floor. He turned his attention to his nephew and jumped up. He picked him up and ran to the kitchen sink, where he tried rinsing his mouth out. Jason wasn't getting any better. His crying grew louder, and then he started holding his stomach, all the while crying his lungs out. Ravon sat him down and tried to think. Jason wobbled a few times before falling down onto the apartment's floor.

Ravon rushed over to his nephew, who was down on all fours, gasping for air. Ravon picked him up and started patting his back, but that only seemed to make it worse. He sat him on the sofa and picked up his phone and dialed 911. He told the paramedics that his nephew had gotten into some rat poison. Once the ambulance arrived, the emergency tech pumped Jason's stomach, which saved his life.

Once the doctor came out and asked for Jason's parent or legal guardian, he explained that it wasn't rat poison her son had ingested and that it was cocaine. A few minutes later, the police showed up, followed by a state social worker.

Ravon owned up to everything and was arrested for child endangerment, but the biggest blow came when the little white social worker told Zola that they were removing Jason from her care until the investigation was complete and that she wouldn't be able to come and see him in the hospital until a decision had been made. She was only 18 years old. She had been living on her own in the projects with a plan to get herself and Jason a better life, but once she realized she was losing her son, she all but gave up on living.

Zola looked at Ravon as he drove. She had already gone through every emotion possible when it came to him. She wanted to hate him, but she just couldn't.

Ravon seemed to be deep in thought. She reached over and rubbed his leg. "It's okay, Ray."

"How is it okay?"

"It just is," she said as she reached in her purse and pulled out her phone again. She hit a few numbers and dialed Andre's number. Voicemail again. "This idiot isn't answering his phone, and I don't even have enough money to catch a bus home."

"When I talked to Sara, she said that your dude beats you," Ravon said slowly with a dangerous undertone. "You mind talking about that?"

"How would she know?"

"Looking at your face, I would say she might be on to something, Zo," Ravon said.

"I honestly don't know what happened. He has never hit me before, but I'm drawing a blank on this, and I don't know why. But it is driving me crazy."

"You don't know, huh?" Ravon said, shaking his head. "I don't understand you women. You stay with guys who beat you, then make excuses for them or try to protect them."

"I'm not making an excuse. I just don't remember what happened. Turn here," she said, pointing toward the I-20 East marker.

"I'm taking you to the hospital."

"We can go to the hospital later, but I need to go home first," Zola said as she pulled down the passenger-side sun visor and looked at her face. "Oh, my goodness."

"Zo," Ravon said, shaking his head, "you need to see a doctor. Like right now."

"I know, but take me home first."

Chapter 5

Ian walked into the living room, where his father was sitting, and took a seat on the sofa across from him. He took a sip of his coffee and set the mug down on the end table beside him. He rubbed his hands together and took a deep breath, gathering his thoughts. He blew the air from his lungs and shook his head.

Colin didn't say a word.

Ian stared at his father. He realized that he missed their relationship. They were always close, but every time Ian saw him, he couldn't help but think of all the pain from losing his family.

"I was coming home from work," Ian started, but stopped again. He couldn't believe what he had done. Somehow his life just didn't pan out the way he had expected.

Colin didn't push his son. He sat back in his chair and crossed his legs as if they were having a leisurely Sunday chat. Ian looked through the bars of his living room window at the people going to and fro outside on the street. He was trying to find the right words to explain his actions.

"I don't like living over here anymore," he said. "I thought I would like it. Thought I could make a difference around here, but these people don't want to change. They've been living like this so long they don't know how to change."

Colin didn't respond.

"If I'm going to hell, then I might as well experience a little heaven while I'm here on earth. That's if I don't end up in prison."

Colin still didn't say anything.

"Do you know this house has been broken into ten times since we moved in here two years ago? Ten times, Dad. And on top of that, they did it while I was at work. I'm working and they're stealing."

"Son," Colin said, motioning with his hands for Ian to tell him what he came to hear.

"Yes, sir," Ian said. "I was just thinking out loud. That's all."

"Tell me what happened last night," Colin said, cutting to the chase. "I have somewhere to be."

"I'm gonna tell you," Ian snapped. "Will you give me a minute? I'm just trying to tell you what's been bothering me. Do you mind? Can I at least have a decent conversation with my father before I get into any of this other crap?"

"Sure," Colin said. "I apologize. What's on your mind, son?"

Ian sighed again. He was stressed, and it showed in the wrinkles in his forehead. "I was just thinking about moving. I don't want my son growing up looking out of bars that are over his bedroom window."

"Well, move. You can live anywhere you want, Ian. You know that. You were born into wealth. This was your choice to live here. It was your choice to turn away from your family. It was your choice not to use your master's degree and instead to go work with guys with GEDs on a garbage truck. Maybe you figure that's your way of punishing me?"

"No," Ian said with a frown. "Why does everything have to be about you?"

"I'm just asking a question, son."

"Well, no. I don't know what it's about."

"Okay. You're grown, and I'm sure you'll figure it out," Colin said. "I'm always here for you. You're my son, and you'll always be my son."

Ian looked at his father. He was a stern man, a hard man, who had lived a hard life, and he made no apologies about how he earned his living. It seemed the only soft spots in his heart were reserved for women and children.

"It was raining hard last night. I could barely see," Ian started as his mind flashed back to last night.

Ian had just pulled his trash truck into the parking lot. He did his final checks and shut it down. He jumped out and ran into the City of Atlanta Sanitation Department office and turned in his keys. He punched his timecard and slipped it back into his slot.

"Y'all have a good evening," he said to the secretary. He never knew nor asked her name. "I'll see ya in the morning."

"Bye, Ian," she said as she did a quick flick of her tongue and flirted with her eyes.

"I'm sexually harassed every day up in here. I'm filing charges on you tomorrow," he said with a smile.

"Oh, you're wrong for that. But listen," she said seductively, "if I'm going to get fired, then I think we should sneak off into one of these offices and make it worth my while."

Ian shook his head and fanned her off. He threw his jacket up over his head and ran from the building. He ran hard to avoid the pouring rain and jumped into his Ford Explorer. He turned the ignition, and it wouldn't catch.

"Come on, man. Not today," he said as he popped the hood and got out of the vehicle. He didn't even bother to cover himself from the rain as he looked under the hood.

"You need some help, brodda?" Walker, one of his coworkers, asked.

"Yeah," Ian said. "I think I need a jump."

"You got batt'ry cables?"

"Yeah," Ian said.

"Me gon' pull 'round," Walker said and pulled his car around so that his was facing Ian's. They hooked up the jumper cables to the cars' batteries. Ian jumped back in and turned his ignition. After a few stalls, it started.

"Thanks, man," Ian said. He jumped out and shook Walker's hand. "I owe you one, my friend."

"No mention it," Walker said, shaking his head. "It's no big deal. I like to help. Hey, Ian, you got a second?"

"Yeah," Ian said as he ran around Walker's car and got in the passenger side.

"It's 'bout to start getting colder out'chere. You might wanna look into replacing dat old batt'ry, brodda."

"Yeah, I think I'ma run by Pep Boys on the way home. What's on your mind, big man?"

Walker sighed and shook his black face. He seemed to be hurting inside. He looked down at his long fingers and rubbed his wedding ring.

Walker's real name was Dabab Lulubo Abdullah. He was born and raised in Sudan and spoke with a heavy African accent. He was also almost seven feet tall and walked with a pronounced limp, an injury he suffered fighting in the Sudanese war when he was just a child. Walker fled to America when he was 18 years old with the help of American aid workers to avoid the bloodshed that had plagued his homeland for as long as he could remember. Walker took a liking to Ian because the quiet man never made fun of him like the others and seemed to be an intelligent man. The others only seemed to be into having fun and laughing their lives away, so Walker stayed clear of them and latched on to Ian.

*"I need to get on out of here, but I need some advice
from you, brodda."*

"What's up?" Ian said.

"My wife may be cheating on me."

"What makes you think she's cheating on you, Walker?"

*"She doesn't wanna have intercourse no more. Been
two weeks. Two loooong weeks, brodder, and I'm 'bout
to die. I didn't get married to sleep alone."*

*"So because she doesn't want sex, you think she's
cheating?"*

"Yes," Walker said emphatically.

*"Is she hanging out late, getting phone calls, text
messages from men?"*

*"No," Walker said, shaking his head. "But women
sneaky creatures, brodda. We can't outsmart dem. No
way in hell."*

*Ian chuckled. "So just because she stopped wanting
sex, you think she's cheating?" he asked again.*

*"Women need it too, brodda, and if she's not getting
it from me, den what am I supposed to t'ink?" Walker
asked, frowning so much that his bald head wrinkled.*

*"Walker, y'all have four kids. And you are only what?
Twenty-six? How old is she?"*

"Twenty-four."

"The woman might be tired," Ian said with a smile.

"You t'ink so?"

*"Perhaps. Is that the only reason you think she's cheat-
ing?"*

*"Yeah," Walker said. "I need good loving every night,
man."*

*Ian smiled. "That good loving every night may not be
so good to your wife. Stop being selfish."*

*"Okay," Walker said, nodding his head. "You know
deese American women. I don't. In my country, a
woman doesn't have de option to tell her husband no in
de bedroom. Dat's grounds for an ass whippin'."*

"Well, you are in America now, and women are very different. Especially black women. Trust me! You will get your own ass whipped."

"Negative."

"Okay."

"Man, she got me taking college classes at night over at de college. Said I can't be a trashman my whole life, but I make more money dan her. She's a teacher wit' two diplomas from universities."

"If that's all you have to worry about, then I don't think she's cheating," Ian said, smiling at his friend.

"You t'ink? Good. But hey, she lazy, too, man. Don't wanna work both shifts with de children. You know we got dem twins, and dey just turned two. Terrible twos, brodda, and I mean dey terrible, ya hear me? Tear up every damn t'ing in the house," Walker said, smiling from ear to ear. "I swear, Ian, they'll tear up a nail if given de opportunity."

Ian laughed and shook his head. He could tell his friend loved every minute of his family.

"I like being married, Ian. I really do. But my wife is the pits. You are one lucky man. To be single," Walker said as if he could savor the freedom he once had.

Ian's smile faded. He'd give anything to have his wife back in his life, but none of his coworkers knew much about his past. "Well, Walker, I need to run. Besides, we need to get out of this rain. Take care of them babies and give your wife a break. It's tough handling two two-year-olds along with two other kids. And you guys have all boys?"

"Yeah," Walker said. "Strong sperm run in my tribe, brodda. I'll see you tomorrow, my friend."

Ian got out of Walker's car and back into his truck. He pulled out of the parking lot and onto the access road. He drove slowly because he couldn't see very far in front of him. He made his way to I-285 and merged onto I-20. He got off on Moreland Avenue and made a right at the exit and headed to Pep Boys, where he purchased a battery and some air fresheners. He walked back outside and removed the old battery and installed the new one right there in the parking lot. He jumped back into his SUV and was happy when it started up without a fuss. He eased out of the parking lot and turned back onto Moreland, headed back to I-20. Just as he turned the radio up, out of nowhere, a woman ran out into the street and stopped right in front of his truck.

He slammed on the brakes so he wouldn't run her over. Once his vehicle stopped, he slammed his gear shift into park and jumped out to see what was going on. The woman had dropped to her knees right there in the middle of the street.

"Are you okay?" he asked.

"Help me," she said in a weak voice.

People blew their car horns at Ian, and some gave him the finger as they rode by. He ignored them and leaned down to help the woman to her feet. She seemed to be pretty young, maybe 25 but no older than 30. She was bleeding from her mouth, and the area around her eyes was puffy and discolored.

"Can you stand?" Ian asked.

"Yes," the woman said, looking around dazed and confused.

Is she high? he wondered.

All of a sudden, the woman let out an ear-piercing scream and used what little strength she had to clutch his arm. Ian turned his head to see what she was so afraid of, and what he saw startled even him. A tall and well-built man came at the woman with the aggression of a lion stalking his prey.

"*Mind your fucking business, potna. This is my bitch. Bought and paid for,*" *the big man said as he reached out and grabbed the woman as if she were an unruly child.* "*Get yo' ass back in that damn house. What the hell is your problem? Have you lost your damn mind? Running out in the street like some stray cat.*"

Ian felt the woman trying to place something into his hand as the big man was pulling at her.

A set of keys.

Ian took them and eased them into his pocket before the big man could see what had just happened. The man grabbed a handful of her hair and dragged her out of the street, barely missing being hit by a passing car. The big man stopped and held up a fist to the passing driver as he stepped up on the sidewalk. He turned around and gave Ian one last warning look.

Ian stared at the couple. The woman didn't take her eyes off of him. She was pleading with her swollen eyes for him to help, but he just stood there. He had to do something, but what? Nothing irked him more than a coward, and a man who would hit a woman, under any circumstance, was a true coward in his book. Yet standing there in the rain doing nothing, it was he who felt like the coward.

Ian knew right then and there that he wasn't going to leave that woman alone. He couldn't just get in his truck and go on about his business knowing that there was someone out there who he could've helped. And since God set his day up so that he would be right here, right now, she was his business.

Ian stood there in the pouring rain, unable to take his eyes off the poor woman who was doing everything except begging him to help her.

"*Hey, man,*" *he yelled,* "*leave that woman alone.*"

"Or what? What you gonna do about it?" the man growled and swung a big silver pistol up and pointed it at Ian. "Come on and play Captain Save a Ho, and I'll drop you where you stand."

"Big tough guy with a gun. Put it down and deal with me like a man," Ian said.

"You better get on about ya business, potna," the big coward said as he turned away.

"Put the gun down. You're tough. Tough enough to beat a woman. Come try that with me," Ian said, trying to keep the man from taking the woman out of his sight, but to no avail. The coward ignored him and dragged the woman out of sight and into the parking garage.

Ian couldn't believe what he was witnessing at seven o'clock in the evening. The streets were still filled with people, yet nobody said or did a thing. The people hurried by or kept driving as if they couldn't see what was happening. The poor woman was alone in a city full of people. He took a deep breath and walked back to his truck and got in. He didn't move. He found his cell phone and dialed 9 and 1 but couldn't bring himself to dial the other 1. People stood on their horns, urging him to move out of their way, but he just sat there.

"Oh, give it a break. Woman is out here getting her brains beat out and y'all in a rush to go do what?" he said to no one in particular.

He looked in his rearview mirror, and an old white man was behind him, blaring his horn nonstop. He got out of his truck and walked toward the man. He stopped at his door, but the man wouldn't look at him. He knocked on the window, but the man kept looking straight ahead, still sitting on the horn. Ian snatched open the man's door.

"Stop blowing your damn horn or I will snatch your old ass out of this car and beat the shit out of you."

The old man slammed his car in reverse, not caring if he hit anyone. He hit his brakes and put his car back in drive and sped around Ian's truck.

"You should've done that the first time, asshole," Ian said, walking back to his vehicle. His thoughts went back to the woman. He looked at the building that the man had dragged the woman toward, and he counted the floors. It was a four-story building: three were used for living space, and the bottom level was for the garage. He put on his signal light and turned into the garage.

He pulled into a parking space, put his truck in park, and pulled out his cell phone. He called his babysitter and told her that he would be a little late and that he would take care of the extra cost once he arrived. Once he hung up the phone, he sat there. Waiting. He wasn't sure what he was waiting for, but he knew he had jumped into this mess headfirst. He reached into his glove compartment and removed his gun. He hated guns but knew in this crazy world sometimes you had to fight fire with fire. Ian stepped out of the truck and slipped the gun against the small of his back, beneath his belt.

Ian got out of his truck and surveyed his surroundings. He listened for sounds of the battered woman as he slowly walked toward the door leading into the building. There was an elevator right beside the glass doors. He decided to take the elevator. He pushed the number two button and waited as he was lifted to the floor. He stepped off and walked down the hallway. He stopped and placed his ear to the first door, only staying a few seconds so he didn't look too suspicious. He moved on to the next door and did the same thing. He walked the entire hallway doing that yet didn't hear anything out of the ordinary: a few television sets, kids crying, some loud music. He even heard a couple making love, but nothing out of the ordinary.

After checking every door, he mad
staircase and walked up to the next j
the same routine of listening at the doo
hear anything out of the ordinary on this floor
he hit the stairwell again. He was on the top flo
walked down the hall doing the same thing. After che
ing four doors, he heard what he was there for. The big
man's voice boomed, but he didn't hear the woman. He
stood outside the door, listening with his ear to the door.
A young white girl with long blond hair was walking
down the hallway toward him. She had on headphones
and seemed to be in her own world.

Ian fiddled around with the key the woman had given
him and acted as if he were looking for his cell phone.
The white girl stopped and opened the door next to the
one he was standing in front of. He slid the key into
the lock, and before he opened the door, he snuck a peek
back at the white girl, and she looked right into his eyes.
He couldn't turn back now. He opened the door and
walked in.

The man from the street stood with his back to him
and obviously didn't hear him enter his domain. The
big man had on the same blue shirt he had on outside,
but his pants were down by his ankles as he yelled
obscenities at the woman as his hips gyrated back and
forth. There was no doubt he was having sex with her,
but the woman didn't make a sound.

Ian walked up behind the man, who was wrapped up
in his deviant sexual act. Ian was close enough to touch
him. He removed his pistol and placed it at the back of
the man's head.

"I'm the man," the big man said as he had sex with
the woman. "And you need to learn how to stay in your
place. You gonna run out on me? I'll teach you."

Fifteen years of karate lessons were all coming down to this. Ian slid his gun back where he had it and tapped the man on his shoulder. Startled, the man made a girlish scream and jumped. When he turned around, his eyes registered instant fear. With all of his force, Ian punched the man with the heel of his right palm. The blow hit the big man under his nose and forced it up, causing a hideous cracking sound. The man opened his mouth, but nothing came out. Ian struck him in his neck, and the man's hands flailed as he tried to break his own fall.

Ian never made a sound as he pounced on the man. He kicked him in his groin, and the man gave up. His eyes were wet with moisture as he lay there on the cold stone floor of the high-priced condominium, half naked and beaten half to death. The man's eyes rolled into the back of his head as if he were begging for the angel of death to come take him away from the obvious pain he was in.

Ian looked at the woman. She was still bent over the sofa with her rear end exposed. He tried to lift her, but she was dead weight. He looked back over at the big man, who was trying to pull his pants up as if he wanted to die with a little dignity.

Ian stood still. He couldn't move. No one was moving. The woman was still lying over the edge of the sofa as if she were asleep. The big man was on the floor, staring up with dead eyes.

Ian shook the woman. She wasn't moving. He checked her pulse and found one. He pulled up her pants and lifted her up. He looked around and saw her purse and coat sitting on the chair. He hurried over and grabbed the purse and the coat. He lifted the woman up as if she were a baby and hurried out of the condo. He walked down the hallway to the stairwell and quickly made it back to the garage.

He shook the woman to try to wake her, but she was in bad shape. He thought about driving her to a hospital and dropping her off but thought that was a bad idea. He went through her purse and found a driver's license. He realized the address wasn't the one they had just left. He punched the address in his navigation system and followed the instructions until he was at a house in the hood.

Ian turned to his father, who was still sitting with his legs crossed and his hands on his knees, just as cool as ever.

"I see," Colin said.

"Now what?" Ian asked.

"You should use your head a little more before you act next time."

"I did use my head. Thanks to you, I don't feel comfortable calling the police."

"There you go, Ian. Blame your troubles on anybody but the man in the mirror. You can call the police just like anybody else, but you would rather soak in your misery. I lost just as much as you lost in that bowling alley, but life goes on. I hate to sound cold, but you're going to have to snap out of this depression, son. You have a son to raise, but you have him living over here in squalor all because you're mad at me. Well, that's smart."

"I'm not mad at you, Dad," Ian said as a tear made its way down his cheek. "I just can't get over the fact that my family is gone."

"Your family is not gone. You have a beautiful son, a sister, a brother, and I'm still here. Are things perfect? No, but they're better than you're allowing them to be."

Ian nodded while looking at the hardwood floor. "How did you know about last night?"

Colin didn't answer. He stood, took a deep breath, and walked over to peek in on his grandson. "Always think of him first," Colin said, turning around to face his son. "You did a very dangerous, not to mention stupid, thing, Ian. That wasn't your business."

"So what now?" Ian asked, wringing his hands just as he did when he was a child and found himself in a situation where he needed his father to fix his mess.

"Now," Colin said, "I'll take care of it. Just go on about your business as if this whole incident never happened."

"But I killed a man," Ian said.

Colin gave him a side-eyed look, reminding Ian that this wasn't his first kill and that he took care of it then and he would do the same this time.

"Your sister is cooking dinner on Friday. I expect you to be there. It's time you come out of your hole and rejoin the world."

Chapter 6

Zola was lost in a daze. She really needed to see a doctor, but something was pulling her to go home. She needed to get a grip on things as soon as possible or risk going completely crazy. She told Ravon to get off on the Moreland Avenue exit and to keep straight. They got caught at a red light, and as they waited for the light to change at Memorial Drive, Zola noticed something. She was looking at a man who was pumping gas into a black pickup truck. There was something about the man that held her attention. She scanned him up and down. He was wearing a green work shirt with matching pants, black work boots, and a pair of white work goggles perched on his head. She wondered why he wasn't wearing a coat. Her eyes burned into the man's face, but he didn't look familiar. So why was she staring at him so hard? There was something about this man that was calling her name.

The light changed, and she was tempted to ask her brother to pull into the station, but she decided not to. They drove along Moreland, passing through an area that was in the midst of gentrification. The poor residents were being forced out by the dozens and replaced by the buppie crowd. On one corner, they passed a dilapidated house, and on the next, a high-price condominium was being built.

"Stop," she said just as she remembered something that might lead her to an answer to one of the many questions bouncing around her head. "Pull over right here."

"Zo, I can't just pull over in the middle of the street," Ravon said, looking in his rearview mirror for clearance.

"Just stop," Zola said as she pulled at the door handle.

"Wait a second," Ravon said as he maneuvered the Honda out of the street and into the parking lot of Chase Bank.

Zola got out of the car and walked over toward the sidewalk. She stopped and stood there. Something about this spot was calling her name. What was it? She remembered being in the street and screaming, but she couldn't put the rest of the pieces of the puzzle together.

Ravon got out of the car and walked over to her. "You okay, Zo?"

"I'm not sure what I am, Ray," she said, confused and pointing at the busy avenue. "I was out in this street. I think I got hit by a car, but I just can't remember what the hell happened."

"Hit by a car?" Ravon asked with a frown. "What makes you think you got hit by a car, Zo?"

"I remember lying down in that street. That much I do remember," she said, scratching her head, trying to force the memories back. "But what was I doing in the street?"

"And you think whoever hit you was the one who took you over to Sara's?"

Zola shook her head. "I don't know, but I know I was in that street. This is as weird as it comes, man. I know I'm not crazy, but I just can't remember anything."

"Are you okay?" Ravon asked as he placed a hand on his sister's shoulder.

"No," Zola said, looking around and taking a deep breath. "I'm not sure what I am, Ray. But something happened to me right here."

Ravon walked her back over to the car and helped her into her seat. He walked back around and jumped in the driver's seat and turned to his sister. "Zo," Ravon said.

"I'm here for you. You don't have to fight this thing alone. If there is anything I can do for you, let me know."

"Thanks," Zola said, but her mind was still racing.

They pulled out of the bank's parking lot and back onto Moreland. Then, less than one hundred yards from the bank, Zola told him to turn into an underground garage. They parked and got out of the car. Zola placed her purse on the hood of the car while she searched for her keys. She dug all around her big Coach duffle bag but couldn't find them.

"Okay," she said, frustrated. "Now where are my keys?"

Ravon stood, staring at his sister, not knowing what to think. He hated every misdeed that was ever leveled against her. His heart ached for her, and he made a vow to do whatever he had to do to lighten her load.

"I need to run into the front office and get a key. Come on."

They walked through the glass double doors and into the eclectic lobby of Select Condominiums. The builders spared no expense when constructing the living quarters. Marble and glass were everywhere, from the floors to the ceiling. One of the largest leather sofas known to man sat facing an equally large fireplace. On the opposite wall was a huge fish aquarium, which faced the street, so anyone passing by could see sharks and small dolphin as well as the blue, yellow, green, and orange fish. The aquarium was filled with all kinds of weird yet exotic-looking aquatic wildlife.

"Hi there, Zola. How are you doing today?" Kecia, the receptionist, said as her face registered the shock she felt when she took in Zola's swollen face.

Kecia White was in her early twenties and was as pretty as a baby. Her deep chocolate skin was flawless. She had large, sleepy eyes that reminded Zola of a doe. She kept her hair in a short natural and had it faded on the sides. Kecia worked at the condo as a means to help pay her way through law school. She was as on the ball as anyone Zola had ever met. Her easy smile and comforting demeanor never let on about her rough-and-tumble past.

If you didn't know any better, you would think Kecia was born with a silver spoon in her mouth, but she came up on the hard streets of Brooklyn, New York. She had no recollection of her prostitute mother because she was killed by one of her johns before Kecia's first birthday. Her father was an unknown, which meant he was probably one of the many men who roamed Brooklyn's streets searching for a cheap thrill between the legs of women who had lost all hope of ever being anything in life. Kecia was raised by her mother's pimp and his stable of raggedy-looking prostitutes. The women took care of her basic necessities such as food, clothes, and shelter, but that was about it. Knowing the legal age of consent in the state of New York was 17, she made sure to take summer school classes so she could graduate from high school by her seventeenth birthday. She didn't want to take any chances of her mother's pimp suggesting that she become a part of the street life.

On the day of her high school graduation, she packed her bags and walked to the Greyhound bus station and purchased a ticket to Atlanta. Once the bus made it to the station, she caught a cab to Spelman College and met a blessing. As luck or fate would have it, she bumped into one of her favorite authors, Pearl Cleage. Kecia shared her story with Pearl, and the author/lecturer worked her magic. Not only did Pearl get Kecia accepted into Spelman, but she also took care of her living situation while she was in school by inviting her to live with her and her husband, Zaron, until she could secure housing on campus.

With Pearl's help and mentorship, Kecia graduated near the top of her class after three years and jumped right into the law school program at Emory University.

"Hi, Kecia," Zola said. "I've been better, but how are you?"

Kecia kept her professional demeanor, but her eyes betrayed her. One thing that Zola found out about Kecia in their many talks was that the girl knew how to mind her own business. No matter how many times she tried to get some gossip started with Kecia, the girl never fed into it.

"I lost my key," Zola said as if this were just another day. "Don't ask me how, but it's gone."

Kecia nodded and pulled out a log. "No problem. Just sign right here, and I'll run and grab you the spare. You know it needs to be returned within twenty-four hours, right?"

"Now I do," Zola said with a slight smile, which still hurt her lip.

"Cool. Just letting you know because they charge like two hundred dollars or something like that. I'll be right back," Kecia said as she stood and walked behind a wall.

"Damn, Zo," Ravon said. "I hate to be selfish, because I know you wanna get to your place and lie down, but that chick is off the chain. Make the introduction?"

"Awww," Zola said, scratching her temple as if she were really thinking about it. "No."

"Why?"

"Because she's about her business, and she's out of your league. Plus, you have a woman. Stop being a typical man."

"What's my league?"

"Hood rats."

"That's not true. I'm a changed man, Zo," Ravon said. "And how you gonna call my girl a hood rat?"

"Hush, Ravon."

Ravon fanned her off and walked over to the wall-length saltwater aquarium. He was completely amazed at the size of the tank and that it had all forms of colorful and exotic aquatic life swimming around. "Look at this thing, Zo. I know this cost at least twenty-five grand. I wonder if I can steal it."

Zola shook her head. "Changed man, huh?"

"I'm just saying. Y'all got a mini Georgia Aquarium up in this joint."

"Yeah," Zola said, nodding. "It's very relaxing. Sometimes I come down here at night just to read and watch the fish swim around. Their only worry is when they will eat."

"Hell, that's most people's worry," Ravon said. "But not y'all. This is what you call living. Damn, I gotta get my act together."

"Since you're changed now, I'm sure you'll be back on track in no time," Zola said. "My head is killing me."

"I can still take you to the hospital," Ravon said as he ran his finger across the soft leather of the sofa. "Damn, sis, you done came up."

"Not really," Zola sighed.

Kecia came back with the key, and Zola signed for it.

"Thanks, and I'll be sure to get this back to you before my time expires," Zola said.

"No problem," Kecia said, handing Zola the key, but before she released it, she said, "I take a few days off, and I come back and . . . well, I hope you'll call me if you need anything."

"How are you doing today?" Ravon said, interrupting the sisterly moment. "I'm Zola's brother."

"How are you, Zola's brother?" Kecia asked as her eyes lingered on Zola.

"My name is Ravon," he said as he waved his hand to get her attention. "I'm over here."

"Nice to meet you, Ravon," Kecia said, slowly turning to face him.

Ravon reached out his hand to her and was met with a firm handshake in return.

"Maybe we can exchange numbers or something," Ravon said. "You are probably one of the sexiest women I've ever seen."

"Thank you for the compliment, but I'm going to have to pass on the number exchange," Kecia said as she took her seat and turned her attention back to her computer. "Anyway, I need to get back to work."

"Oh, it's like that?" Ravon said with a frown.

"Like what?"

"You're blowing me off. I guess I don't have the look for your type, huh?"

Kecia gave him a condescending smile as if he were a little boy with a crush on his grade school teacher.

"Wow," Ravon said. "Black women."

"Black women?" Kecia said, looking up. "What's wrong with black women?"

"Y'all attitudes suck. Here I am trying to be respectful," he said, "and all you can do is ignore me."

"And I was respectful to you. I'm just not interested."

"Why?" Ravon asked.

"Because I don't have to be," Kecia said.

"I guess I'm not your type, huh?"

"Nobody's my type right now, Ravon. I'm in school, and I don't need any distractions. Is that okay with you?"

"Nope," Ravon said with a frown. "I wanna take you out, prove to my parole officer that I'm running with a different crowd."

"Oh, Lord," Kecia said, laughing. She looked at Zola for some help.

"Come on, boy," Zola said, shaking her head. She grabbed Ravon by his arm and led him to the elevator.

"Have a good day, guys," Kecia said and turned back to her work.

Zola and Ravon got on the elevator, and Zola hit the button with the Roman numeral IV on it. There was a slight jerk, and then the doors opened at the fourth floor. Just as they stepped out of the elevator, they saw a police officer walking toward them.

The officer, a short and stocky white guy with a buzz cut, stopped right in front of Zola's door and waited for them.

"May I help you?" Zola asked.

The officer inspected Zola's condition and frowned. "Ma'am, do you live in this building?"

"Yes, I do," Zola said.

"Were you here last night, let's say around eleven o'clock?"

"No, I wasn't," she said. "You're standing in front of my door."

"Mind if I ask where you were?" he asked with a skeptical look on his face.

"Why?"

"There was a robbery that took place last night next door to you, and I was just wondering if you saw anything," he said.

"No," Zola said. "Like I said, I wasn't here."

The officer gave Ravon a once-over from head to toe, and then nodded his head. "May I ask what happened to your face?"

"I fell down," she said.

"I see," he said as if he knew she was lying. "Y'all have a good day."

Zola placed the key in the lock and turned the knob. Once inside, she paused. It was as if the beating was coming back to her. She could see Andre dragging her around the condo by her hair. She shook the visual from her head and walked into the kitchen. The place was spotless, yet she remembered the kitchen being tossed around pretty good. Plates and canisters were all over the floor. She specifically remembered the ceramic cookie jar breaking as she was being dragged down the counter. She walked over to where she kept it, and the jar was gone. She opened up the pantry door and looked in the trash can, but there was a fresh bag in there.

Zola stopped and scratched her head. Then she ran to the guest room closet. She flung open the door, but there was nothing inside. That was where Andre had kept his clothes, and now there was no sign of him.

"The key," Zola said, turning to her brother.

"What key?" Ravon said, perplexed.

"I gave my key to this man I met on the street. He stopped to help me, and I gave him my key. Oh, my God."

Ravon frowned. "Stopped to help you? Who stopped to help you? And what was he helping you do?"

"This man," she said. "I remember running, and Andre was chasing me. Then this man stopped his truck, and I gave him my key." She walked around the two-bedroom condo, looking for signs of anything that would help jar her memory. "I wonder where he is," she said.

"Who?"

"Andre."

"Me too. I really need to meet this punk-ass nigga who decided to put his hands on you. Maybe I can ask him if he'd like to try that shit on me."

"It's not like that."

"Not like what?"

"Like what you think."

"What am I thinking?"

Zola ignored him and walked over to the living room. She was looking around as if she were a crime scene investigator. Things were coming back to her now, and the more she remembered, the more she wished that she'd never met Andre.

The pain in her side shot a debilitating jolt to her, and she winced and took a seat on the sofa.

"Zo," Ravon said, "what's going on?"

"What do you mean?" Zola asked, and she rubbed her side gingerly.

"What's going on here? Who is this Andre guy?"

"Just a guy I know."

"Is this his place?"

"No," she said. "It's mine."

"Where do you work?"

"I don't."

"Then how can you afford a place like this?"

"Long story," she said.

"I got time."

"He bought it, but it's my place. My name is on the deed."

"And he gets to come around here and beat your ass when he feels like it? Is that part of the deal?"

If you only knew, she thought but kept her mouth closed. "It's not like that," Zola said.

"Stop saying that! What is it like then?" Ravon snapped.

Zola didn't respond. She pulled out her cell phone again and dialed Andre's number.

"Hello," said a man's voice that didn't belong to Andre.

"Hello," Zola said. "May I speak to Andre?"

"No," the man's voice said.

"Who is this?" she asked.

"Zola," the voice said, "I want you to listen to me and listen very carefully."

"Who in the hell is this?"

"I'm talking," the voice said calmly.

Zola didn't respond. There was something about the man's tone that said he meant business.

"I want you to forget you ever met Andre. If anyone happens to ask you any questions about Andre, you are to tell them the truth. And the truth is you haven't seen him since the last time he attacked you. Now if you don't and insist on asking questions, things can get bad for you in a hurry. Pretty simple—you keep your mouth closed and live, or run your mouth and it gets ugly. It's totally up to you."

"Who is this?"

"You're running your mouth," the voice said. "Now hang up the phone and enjoy your life."

Zola dropped her head. *What have I gotten myself into?* she wondered and pushed the little red icon to end the call. She looked at her brother. "This shit is getting weirder by the minute."

Chapter 7

Ian rode on the back of the garbage truck, lost in his thoughts. Walker was rambling on about something or other, but Ian wasn't hearing him. It had been a full week since he entered that man's condominium and killed him. Surprisingly he wasn't worried about the repercussions of that crime anymore. There was something about his father getting involved that washed away any fear he had of going to jail. The only thing that bothered him now was the woman. He couldn't stop thinking about her, and he wanted to know if she was okay. Did she survive? She was beaten pretty badly, and she was unconscious when he dropped her off. The more he thought about it, the more he wished he had taken her to a hospital instead of dropping her off on a porch somewhere in the middle of the hood. He did find a little comfort in the fact that whoever answered the door did get her into the house.

Ian had driven by that same house where he dropped the woman off at least ten times, but he couldn't bring himself to get out of his truck and knock on the door.

Just then, his cell phone rang. Ian looked at the caller ID. It was his sister, Andrea.

"Hello," he said, pushing the phone close to his ear so that he could hear over the noise of the garbage truck. "How's life treating you?"

"I've been better," she said. "What about you?"

"What's wrong?" he asked.

"The question is, what's wrong with you? I'm worried about you," she said. "You don't spend time with us no more. You keep my nephew away from me, and that's just not fair. I love him more than you give me credit for, but you won't let me or anyone else see him. That's selfish and uncalled for."

Ian held the phone to his ear. His sister had always been a drama queen, but she had a point. "I'll make sure I do a better job of staying in touch."

"You always say that and nothing changes. No," Andrea said. "That's not gonna fly this time."

"What do you want me to do, Andrea?"

"I'm cooking dinner tonight, and I want you guys to come over. Everyone will be here, including Daddy."

"I heard. What's the occasion?" he asked.

"It's a surprise. Besides, why does it have to be a special occasion for family to get together?"

"It doesn't have to be anything special. I was just asking."

"I'm just happy to have a family, and I want to see you guys more often. So I'm not taking no for an answer. I expect to see you and Christian."

"I don't know," he said. "I've had a long week. Maybe another time."

"Who hasn't had a long week, Ian? Come on. This would mean a lot to me. Malcolm is flying in from Seattle for the weekend. There, now you ruined the surprise."

"When did he move to Seattle?"

"Last year, Ian."

"Wow. I guess I'm out of the loop."

"Well, get back in it. Are you gonna come?"

Ian was quiet for a minute. He needed to get a life, and maybe he could start with his family. "Yeah," he said. "We'll be there."

"Yayyyyy," she screamed as if she were a child on a roller coaster at an amusement park. "I can't wait. I haven't seen Christian since this past summer."

"Yeah," Ian said. "It has been a while."

"I'm so looking forward to it. I'll see you around seven, okay?"

"That works for me. See you tonight," he said before hanging up.

"Who dat you talkin' to, brodda? Some pretty girl?"

"Yeah," Ian said with a smile. "She's just lovely."

"Good for you, brodda. You gotta release your testicles every so often or you'll blow up and die. For true," Walker said, nodding rapidly to support his African myth.

Ian laughed.

"It's not a laughing matter. My wife said no more sex for two months. I feel like a dead man walking. If God didn't want you to use it, why would He put so much fire in de body? I'm going to get a girlfriend. De kind you pay money for. Dat way all of my problems will go away, and I don't have to worry about getting a divorce. If Tiger Woods weren't so cheap, he might be okay."

"Didn't you just accuse your wife of cheating? How you gonna go out and cheat?"

"In my country a man cannot cheat. As long as he can afford her, he's good to go, and I can afford a woman on de side, brodda."

"Well, in this country that'll get your dick chopped off," Ian said.

Walker frowned and instinctively grabbed his private part and almost fell off the back of the truck. Ian laughed again. It felt good to be laughing. It felt like he hadn't laughed so freely in years.

They pulled into Lake Kanawha, one of Atlanta's most expensive neighborhoods, and started emptying the trash cans. After they cleared about five or six houses, a man called out to them as he ran dragging a can behind him. Ian hit the side of the truck to get the driver to stop.

Ian recognized him immediately, but the man didn't seem to know who he was. He stared directly into the eyes of the man he thought he had killed.

Confused, Ian peered in for a closer look. Was his mind playing tricks on him? No, this was the guy. He never forgot a face, and he was 100 percent sure this was the same guy, but the big man looked perfectly fine. No cuts, no bruises, nothing on his face to show that he had just sustained a serious beatdown a few days before. And up until this very moment, Ian actually thought he had killed the guy. His mind went back to the scene of the crime, and he visualized the big man lying on the floor with his nose split wide open while he struggled to pull his pants up. That man's nose was bleeding profusely and had a nasty gash on the bridge. At the very least, this man should've had a scratch to show for his troubles, but his face was as smooth as a baby's bottom.

"Hey," the man said, "I'm sorry to hold you guys up, but I forgot today was trash day. I already missed it last week. This crap has been in my garage, and it's starting to stink."

"No problem, brodda," Walker said. "You right on time."

Ian stared at the man and wondered what kind of magical healing herbs he was sipping on. A part of him wanted to jump off the back of the truck and reintroduce himself for the ill deeds he had done to that woman, but the smarter part of him made him simply nod his head when the man made eye contact.

Walker took the can from the man, emptied it, and handed it back to him.

"Have a blessed day, fellas," the man said with an easy smile as if he were the nicest man in the world. He reached into his pocket and removed his wallet.

Walker smiled, but Ian couldn't stop thinking about how this guy pointed a gun at him in the middle of a busy street after beating a woman half to death.

"I'm glad I caught you. I sure didn't want to spend a few more days with this stench in my garage, so I appreciate you waiting. And I know time is money, so . . ." he said and removed two $20 bills. He handed them to Walker.

"Thank you, my brodda," Walker said, slipping the money in his pocket and jumping back on the truck. "God loves a cheerful giver."

"Y'all take care of yourselves," the man said and turned and jogged back up his driveway.

The truck pulled off, and Ian watched as the big man disappeared back into the garage of a high-priced home. He couldn't help but wonder if he had a wife and kids inside the tony home. He bet she had no idea he was running around across town beating up women.

"Here ya go," Walker said, handing him one of the twenties. "Nothing makes my day like generosity."

"You go ahead and keep that, Walker," Ian said, still staring at the man's home.

"You must be wealthy, brodda. I don't turn down nuttin' but my collar," Walker said as he laughed and put the money back into his pocket.

Ian made a mental note of the man's address. He kept his eye on the trash bag and wondered what was inside. He knew this wasn't his business and he should just leave it alone, but that wasn't going to happen. He was coming back.

Chapter 8

After lying around her condo for four days, Zola realized she wasn't getting any better. Rest alone wasn't going to heal her. She reached for her cell phone and dialed her brother's number.

"Yo, this is your boy, Ravon. I'm on my grind right now, but leave me a message and I will holla back." *Beep.*

"Ravon," Zola said, barely able to speak, "this is Zola. I need you to take me to the hospital. You know I can't do ambulances."

She hung up the phone and grimaced as she swung her legs over the side of the bed. She stood up and felt a little dizzy.

The sun was peeking around the blinds and into her bedroom. She looked at the clock, and it was already nine o'clock in the morning. She found her balance and walked to the bathroom. With each step she took, it felt like someone was stabbing her in the ribs with a long needle. She sat down on the toilet to relieve herself, but something didn't feel right. As Zola looked down between her legs, what she saw down in the water almost scared the life out of her.

The toilet bowl was now a crimson red as her blood splattered all over the white porcelain. Trembling with fear, she stood and moved away from the blood until her back was against the wall. She stared at the blood like it was death itself, then looked up to the ceiling as if God had some answers to the million and one questions running around her head. Zola took a deep breath but felt her stomach turn. She rushed over to the toilet and threw up. Finally able to gain her composure momentarily, she flushed the toilet and walked over to the sink to rinse out her mouth.

Zola made it back to her bedroom and picked up her cell phone. She scrolled through the address book on her BlackBerry and realized that she didn't have anyone she could call. All her associates were either friends of Andre's or people she did business with, such as the dry cleaner, plumber, and hairstylist. She had been completely cut off from any form of a social life since she started dealing with Andre. Finally, out of options, she found the number to the front office and got Kecia on the line.

"Kecia," she said, "this is Zola. I really need your help."

"Hey, Zola. Are you okay? What do you need?"

"I need to go to the hospital," Zola said, hoping she sounded calmer than she felt.

"What's going on? Should I call an ambulance?"

"No, I hate ambulances," Zola said. "I was wondering, could you take me?"

"Okay, sure, but I'll have to find somebody to cover for me. Can you give me a few minutes?" Kecia asked.

"I feel like I'm dying, but I can't get in an ambulance," she managed through bated breath.

"Okay," Kecia said. "Hold tight. I'll be right up."

"Thank you, Kecia. I owe you big time," Zola said. "I'm throwing up and urinating blood."

"Oh, my God. Maybe I *should* call an ambulance, Zola. That sounds serious."

"No, just get here as soon as you can."

"Will do," Kecia said before hanging up.

Less than ten minutes later, Kecia was standing over Zola's bed, looking down at a woman who was barely hanging on. "Oh, my God," Kecia said. "What in the world happened to you?"

Zola struggled to her feet, and Kecia ran over to assist her before she fell down. Kecia helped Zola over to the sofa while she looked around for something for her to wear to the hospital.

"I wish I knew," Zola said, frustrated that after four days she still had little recollection of what had happened.

"Why didn't you call me sooner?"

"I don't know."

"Well, let's get you to a doctor," Kecia said. She found a house robe hanging on the foot rail of the bed and slid it on Zola's fragile body. She looked around and grabbed Zola's purse, then helped her get to her feet.

Somehow, they made it down the hallway, down the elevator, and to Kecia's car. Kecia drove a Mini Cooper, and the passenger seat was filled with clothes, and the already-small rear seat was taken up with two large boxes.

"Oh, doggone it. I forgot I had all of this stuff in my car," Kecia said. "I had to move out of my place last night."

"We can take my car," Zola said as she started walking down the garage toward her Jaguar.

Kecia led Zola over to the car and eased her down into the passenger seat. She closed the door and rushed around to the driver's side and jumped in. After buckling up, she eased out of the parking garage and headed toward Emory University Hospital Midtown.

"Zola," Kecia said as she moved into the HOV lane on I-20 West, "what happened to you? You said you didn't remember, but surely you remember something?"

"I keep hoping this is a bad dream, but I know it's not," Zola said, wincing in pain. She was tired of the pain, and for the first time in a long time, she wished that she were dead.

"I see," Kecia said. "I really like to mind my business. I swear to God I do, because I have enough problems of my own. But when I saw you walk into the lobby the other day . . . my heart just broke into a million little pieces.

"The temp who was working for me a few days ago called and told me she saw you running in the street trying to get away from Mr. Harris. I didn't believe her at first, but then you came in, and I realized she was telling the truth. Before, I always ignored the rumors when other tenants would come down and say how they could hear you screaming when they were walking down the halls. But now . . ."

Zola felt embarrassed to hear these words, but she was in too much pain to really care.

"That's why I was actually happy when those men came to get his ass," Kecia said.

Zola's ears perked up, and she looked at Kecia. "What men?"

"There were three of them. They came to me and got the videotapes from the garage, and then they went and got him. He was crying like a baby, too. Mumbling something about how he would tell them everything. I'm like 'tell them what?' I've been around men like Mr. Harris my entire life. They can give it, but they can't take it."

"What men are you talking about? Who took Andre? Were the men police officers?"

"I don't know, but I don't think so, and after seeing you like this, I really don't care."

Zola thought back to the warning she got from the man who'd called and figured she'd better learn to think like Kecia, or she would find herself in worse shape than she was already in.

"You're gonna be okay, Zola," Kecia said. "We're almost there."

Zola nodded as she let the seat all the way back so that she had less pressure on her aching ribs. Then her cell phone rang.

"You wanna get that?" Kecia asked.

Zola nodded, and Kecia reached into the back seat to retrieve Zola's purse. She fiddled around inside the purse while she used her left hand to steer the vehicle.

"Here," she said, handing the phone to Zola.

Zola looked at the screen, and it said PRIVATE. She hit the green icon. "Hello," she said.

"Hi, Mom," Jason's lively voice said on the other end of the line.

Zola's heart rate increased, and she tried to sit up, but that painful jolt hit her sides, forcing her to stay put. "Hey, buddy," she said, trying to sound as normal as possible. "How are you?"

"I'm good. How are you?"

"Actually, I'm on my way to the hospital."

"Hospital?" Jason asked, sounding more mature than he had the last time they spoke. "Why?"

"I was in a bad car accident," Zola lied.

"Oh, no," Jason said. "Which hospital? I'm going to see if my mom or dad will bring me there to see you."

Zola loved to hear her son's voice on the other end of the telephone, and when he called her Mom, that was even sweeter, but when she heard him refer to another woman as Mom, somehow that bothered her. She had all the respect in the world for the Benjamins. They were very good people, and she really appreciated the fact that they were giving her son a better life than any she could've ever imagined, but she wanted that Mom title to be hers and hers alone.

"I'm going to Emory University Hospital Midtown. I'd love it if you'd come see me."

"I'll try," Jason said. "What happened?"

"A car pulled out in front of me," she said, still lying and hating every minute of it.

"I'll call you back in a little while. Let me get my mom on the phone," he said.

"Okay," she said. "I love you."

"I love you too," he said before hanging up.

"That was my son." Zola smiled, realizing that the mere sound of his voice made her happy to be alive.

Chapter 9

Zola was seen and examined by a doctor not long after she arrived in the emergency room of Emory University Hospital Midtown. The physician recommended that she be admitted right away. She was wheeled to a room on a gurney and given a nightgown to change into. She had a private room and thanked God for her insurance. Moments after she was settled, there was a knock on her door.

"Hey," Kecia said, peeking into the room.

"Hey," Zola said as she pulled the covers up around her neck. "You're still here?"

"Yeah," Kecia said as she walked in the room and stood beside Zola's bed. "Did you think I would just leave you here all alone like that? I'm appalled."

Zola smiled. "Thanks for everything, Kecia. I really appreciate you. Whatever they gave me is working. I'm feeling a little better already."

"Good," Kecia said.

"You don't have to stay here. I know you have better things to do than hang around a hospital with me."

"I'm okay," Kecia said, looking down at her battered friend. "What's the word on your condition?"

"Broken ribs, internal bleeding, and a few other things that I couldn't pronounce," Zola said, shaking her head. "They gave me something for the pain. I see how folks get hooked on prescription meds. I'm feeling nice," she said with a smile. "The doctor said he has to run some more tests, so I may be here for a few days."

"Wow," Kecia said. "I hope you're going to leave him. I don't like to mind other people's business, but since you involved me, I feel like I can state my opinion."

"He's not a bad guy," Zola said.

"What?" Kecia almost screamed. "What does he have to do for you to think he's a bad guy? Kill you?"

"No," Zola said. "You just don't understand."

"You know what, Zola?" Kecia said, shaking her head. "Don't be that chick."

"What chick?"

"That one who makes excuses for a man who whips her ass. Under no circumstance are you to be used as a punching bag."

"I hear ya," Zola said, giving up on explaining anything to her well-meaning friend.

Kecia looked at her and shook her head. She had seen this so many times with the prostitutes she grew up with. "Did you call your brother?"

"Not since I left home. Can you hand me my phone out of my purse?"

Kecia walked over and got the phone. Before Zola could dial the number, she noticed she had five missed calls. She called her voicemail and heard four different messages from Jason. He didn't sound happy when he told her he couldn't make it to the hospital. He then said something that she hadn't heard since he went to live with the Benjamins three years ago. He told her he wanted to come home. "Home" meaning back with her. Zola sat up and dialed the number to the Benjamins' home.

"Hello," Chad Benjamin said.

"Hi, Chad," Zola said. "How are you?"

"I'm well," he said in his ever-chipper voice. "How's life treating you?"

"Not so good. I was in a car accident," she said, continuing the lie.

"Oh, no," Chad said. "Are you going to be okay?"

"I think so."

"Well, if you need anything, please don't hesitate to call," he said with genuine concern. "You know we are here for you."

Zola had always had a great relationship with the Benjamins. They were a white couple, living in a wealthy white world, yet they took in her black child with open arms.

"Thank you," she said. "Is Jason around?"

"No," Chad said. "Carmen took him someplace. I'm not sure where they went."

"Hm. Okay," Zola said. "Well, tell him that I'm at Emory University Hospital Midtown."

"Must've been some accident. Are you sure you're okay?" Chad asked.

"Yeah," she said. "I'll be fine. Jason said he was going to ask Carmen to bring him up here to see me, but then he left a message saying he couldn't come."

"Really?" Chad said. "That's odd. I'll have to get her on the phone to see what's going on."

"I have my cell phone, so if you don't mind, tell him to call me. I would love to hear his voice."

"Okay," Chad said. "I will pass along the message, and you get better soon."

"Thank you," she said and ended the call. She placed the phone on her chest, wondering what was going on with her son.

"Is your son okay?" Kecia asked.

"I hope so. He left me a message and said he wants to come back and live with me."

"Is that a good or a bad thing?" Kecia asked, fishing since she wasn't in the know.

"It's a great thing. I have been trying to get myself together so he could come back home, but something in his voice didn't sound right."

"Do you have any pictures of him?" Kecia asked.

Zola picked up her phone and scrolled through the photos. "He sends me stuff all the time," she said as she handed Kecia her BlackBerry.

"He's handsome," Kecia said, scrolling through the pictures. She stopped at a family portrait with Jason and his adoptive family. "Who are these white people in the picture?"

"Those are the people he lives with," Zola said.

"I know this lady," Kecia said, staring at the white woman with the short red hair. "She looks very familiar. I never forget a face. I don't know where I know her from, but it'll come to me."

"That's Carmen," Zola said, rolling her eyes. "His foster mom. She's always on television. She does something with the school board or something political. I'm not sure. Are you sure you don't have anything to do? I'm enjoying your company, but I don't want to keep you."

"My shift is over, and I don't have class tonight. I need to study, but I also need to find a new apartment. I had to bail out of my place last night. Those Negroes were out there shooting at each other like they live in the Wild West or someplace. The last thing I need is to catch a stray bullet. I have places to be in life, and I refuse to let ghetto Negroes ruin it by shooting me in my head," she said.

"Wow," Zola said.

"Bullets came flying right through my wall. If I had been in the kitchen at the time, I wouldn't be here, or if I were lucky, I would be in the room next door," Kecia said, still studying the face of the white woman on Zola's phone. "I know this woman, Zola, and it's not from television."

"Well, if you think of it, let me know. She's okay. A little judgmental at times, but I think her heart's in the right place."

Kecia hit a few buttons and forwarded the picture to her cell phone. Her lawyer instincts were racing. Something wasn't right, and you could read that all over her face. Once she was done, she handed Zola's phone back to her.

A nurse walked in, nodded at Kecia, then checked the machine that was hooked up to Zola. "No cell phones are allowed. They mess with the radio waves in the sensors," the nurse said as she pushed a few more buttons on the monitor. "Sorry, but you can have your loved ones call you on the room phone."

"Thanks," Zola said. Kecia reached out for the phone, and Zola handed it to her.

The nurse left. Kecia offered the phone back to her, but Zola shook her head. "If my son calls, give him the number off that phone right there. I don't need to have anything breaking that will have me staying here any longer than I already have to be here."

Kecia looked at the room phone and punched the number into her own cell.

"Well, Kecia, you are more than welcome to stay at my place. It's not like I'll be there for a few days. Even if I were, you could still stay," Zola said.

"For real? Cool, because I'm broke as a joke. I do not have the money for another deposit and the first and last months' rent, which is what everybody seems to want," Kecia said.

There was a knock on the door, and then it opened before Zola could say a word. Two plainclothes police officers entered the room. Both of them showed their credentials before speaking.

"Are you Zola Zaire?" the tall white officer asked in an official tone.

"Yes," she said.

Kecia took that as her cue to leave. She squeezed Zola's hand and whispered that she would call her. Zola nodded and waited for her to exit the room. "What's the problem?" she asked.

"We are investigating a murder," the black officer said.

"A murder?" Zola frowned as her heart began to race. "Who was murdered?"

"Sara Zaire was found dead today. She was stabbed thirty-three times," the white officer said with the casualness of someone who was ordering lunch at the local McDonald's.

"What?" Zola said as she tried to sit up. "My mother? You're telling me that my mother was murdered?"

"Yes," the white guy said with little, if any, emotion.

"When?"

"We found her today," the white guy said. "And it is my understanding that you were the last person seen leaving her house. Care to have a few words with us?"

Chapter 10

Ian stepped out of the shower and walked into his modest-sized bedroom. He looked around the small room and sighed. The king-sized bed sat in the middle of the room and left very little space for a dresser and a nightstand. Lately he had been finding everything wrong with his house and neighborhood. Before, nothing mattered. Now the kitchen was too cramped, the closets didn't hold all his clothes, and his son's bathroom was too this or his living room was too that. He looked at a pile of real estate magazines he had picked up but never looked at, then made a mental note to look at a few of them when he made it back home tonight. Maybe he and Christian could go house hunting this weekend.

He was even excited about his dinner tonight with his family. He had practically cut everyone off after the loss of his wife and daughter, but now he felt it was time to move on. He sat on his bed, his body still dripping with waterdrops, wearing only a towel. He picked up his family portrait and stared at his daughter's bright smile. She looked like a miniature version of his wife. Ian's eyes moved over to meet his wife's eyes, and he couldn't help but smile. He loved her with everything he had. He shook his head and refused to allow himself to fall back into the trap of asking God why. That line of thinking never got him anywhere. His gaze shifted back to his little girl, and his smile faded. He missed her, but he had cried so many tears for them that he didn't have any more left. He held the picture up to his lips and kissed it. Instead of placing it back on the nightstand, he opened the drawer and placed it inside. It was time to move on, if not for his own sanity, for Christian's.

He realized that in the process of mourning his family, he wasn't allowing his son to live his life to the fullest. His son had been begging him to teach him how to play basketball, and all he ever did was put it off another day, and that day had yet to come. It was almost as if he and Christian were living in a bubble and the rest of the world didn't really exist. He realized how completely self-centered his actions were, but his mourning wouldn't allow him to get out of his own way and let his child have some fun. But something had to give, and it became painfully clear when he picked Christian up from daycare. Once he shared with his son their plans for the evening, Christian started smiling from ear to ear and talking nonstop about a family he barely knew.

Ian stood and walked over to his dresser and pulled out his undergarments and slid them on. He leaned out into the hallway to sneak a peek at his son, who was already pacing. He was past ready to go.

"Hey, man," Ian said. "You got yourself dressed?"

"Yes," Christian said, standing up to show off his black jeans, a T-shirt with a cartoon character of a large red dog on it, and a fireman's hat.

Any other time, Ian would send him back to his room and make him change his clothes, but he was burying that guy. "You are one sharp dude, Mr. DeMarco," he said, smiling and shaking his head.

Christian frowned as if he wasn't expecting that, then smiled. "I can wear it, Daddy?"

"Sure," Ian said. "I don't see why not. You look good in your fireman's hat."

"Thank you," Christian said before sitting down on the floor to play with his cars.

Ian walked back into his room and picked up the remote control for the television he had sitting on the top of the dresser. He turned the volume up on the news and opened the door of his closet to find something to wear. His eyes jerked toward the screen when he heard what the reporter was saying.

"An Atlanta woman is being questioned regarding the apparent murder of Sara Zaire. The woman in question is being treated at Emory University Hospital Midtown and is recovering from injuries in what authorities are calling a domestic dispute."

Ian's eyes grew big as the woman's face popped up on the screen. He knew that face.

"Authorities are saying the victim lived in this house and that she was the mother of the alleged perpetrator. The woman in question, Zola Zaire, has a history of violence against her mother. Sara Zaire was convicted and spent time in prison for crimes against the very person who is now being questioned in her murder. You heard it first here, and we will continue to keep you updated. I'm Samantha James, Channel Seven News at six."

Ian recognized the house on the television as the same one where he had dropped off the beaten woman. He scratched his head and decided he had done his job. He quickly got dressed, turned the television off, and walked out of the room.

"Let's go, li'l buddy," Ian said.

As Ian and Christian walked out on the front porch, they heard gunshots. Ian pushed his son back into the house and told him to go to his room and lie down. Ian retrieved his own gun from his bedroom and walked back to the living room. He peeked out the window and scanned the street for signs of danger. Could someone be coming for him, or was it just the local thugs being themselves? After a few minutes, he stepped outside and looked around.

The area drunks, Willie and Harry, were standing across the street arguing about something and seemingly oblivious to the gunshots that had just gone off.

"Niggero, Barack Obama ain't the president. The white man just put him up front to shut yo' dumb ass up," Willie said as he took a swig of his liquor straight from the bottle. "George Bush and all them other crackers still running thangs."

"You know you about an ign'ant sumbitch," Harry said, shaking his head. "The white man ain't never gave two stankin' cents about what black folks be talking about. So why all of a sudden would they wanna shut us up? And they damn sure ain't going so far as to make a black man president to shut us up. Give the brother his due. He just outsmarted they asses, and now he in the big house, sitting at the big desk, doing big things."

"First of all, he ain't black, so stop calling him a brother," Willie said.

"You a fool. Obama is black. His daddy is blacker than yo' daddy."

"So the hell what?"

"And guess what else. He looks good in a suit," Harry defended Obama. "I'm happy, damn it."

"Bull crap! He ain't no brother. Him and Tiger Woods got the same shit going on with they bloodlines. The white man ain't gonna give no real nigga that job. Trust me on that one," Willie said.

"I wouldn't trust you with a boiled egg and a sock with no match. Hell, the black man wouldn't give a nigga no job. And you should know, nigga. When the last time you had one? The world don't like niggas, and I don't either. Niggas kill grass."

"You damn right. I'm a nigga and proud of it. But you better watch your damn mouth, Harry," Willie snapped. "I'm about tired of the insults. I'll take this damn sword out and chop your damn head off. Try me."

"Man, you and that rusty-ass sword go to hell."

"Keep on and I'ma put my foot so far in your ass your breath gonna smell like my shoe polish," Willie said.

"Willie," Harry said with a frown, "Negro, if you ever dream about putting your raggedy-ass dick beaters on me, you better wake up and apologize. 'Cause I will knock the pure dee snot outta yo' ass."

"You and what army?" Willie said, taking another drink of his liquor before handing it to Harry.

"What's up, fellas?" Ian said, walking up between the two alcoholics who argued to pass the time every day, all day. "Did y'all see who was out here shooting?"

"Hell no," Willie said. "But I sure wish whoever did it would come around here and put one or two in this fool. Dumb sumbitch."

"I ain't gonna be too many more bitches now," Harry warned. "I'm tellin' you now. Keep it up and it ain't gonna be pretty."

"Man," Ian said with a slight chuckle, "why can't y'all get along?"

"'Cause I can't fool with an ign'ant-ass nigga. I don't like niggas, Ian," Harry said as if he was really frustrated with the man he spent his every waking moment with. "And this one right here might as well be called Chief Nigga."

"What make you any better than me, Harry?" Willie snapped.

"My mind," Harry said, slapping himself hard in the temple. "That's what. I got a degree, fool. I grew up—"

"Oh, shut the hell up," Willie said, cutting him off. "Don't nobody wanna hear about what the hell you used to do. Yo' ass be out here with me every damn day, and I quit school in the eighth grade. You think because you went to some old-ass college two hundred years ago with Frederick Douglass that you better than me?"

"You know what, Ian? It gets on my last nerve to see a black man who won't give another black man his proper due," Harry said. "That's why we can't have shit."

"Ian," Willie said, interrupting Harry, "you seem to be a decent man with a good head on your shoulders. Well, when you ain't walking round here with your ass on your face. But anyway, let me ask you a question. Do you think Barack Obama is really the president?"

"Huh?" Ian asked.

"Huh hell," Willie said. "You heard me, nukka. Or do you think he's just a front man? I believe the white man is still calling the shots."

"Yeah, Willie, he's the president," Ian said, shooting a quick glance back at his house to make sure his son was okay. "And he's smart enough to call his own shots."

"Damn," Willie said, shaking his head from side to side as if he had just heard some grave news.

"I can't believe you even asked somebody that dumb question. It's better to let folks think you're stupid than to open your dumb mouth and remove all doubt," Harry said. "You just don't care who knows how ign'ant yo' ass is, do you, Willie?"

"Both of you sumbitches stupid," Willie said, reaching over to Harry. "Give me my goddamn bottle back."

Ian shook his head. "A'ight, guys. Y'all try to be careful out here," he said as he walked back across the street to his house. He opened the door and called out to Christian. The little boy ran to his father, and they jumped into Ian's truck.

Once he was in the car, Ian switched his radio to the news with hopes of hearing something else about the woman whose face was plastered across his television screen. He didn't know her, but something was telling him that she was getting a raw deal. He was willing to bet his last dollar that the abusive man was the one behind the killing. After all, she was in no condition to even walk, much less kill.

But what about his father? Could one of his people be responsible for this? His father did say that he would take care of it.

Ian quickly tossed the thought from his mind. His father was a lot of things, but reckless wasn't one of them. Especially after the family tragedy that changed them all.

Ian tried to think of something else, but his thoughts kept going back to the woman as he drove. In his mind he could see her sitting in a cell all alone. He felt twinges of fear, guilt, and compassion for her. The probability of the police showing up to talk to him increased dramatically with these new developments, yet that wasn't what bothered him most. He was more concerned about the woman.

"Huh, Daddy?"

Ian's mind raced so much that he didn't realize he was ignoring his son. "What was that, buddy?" he asked.

"Can we spend the night?"

"No, we can't spend the night, but we can stay real late. How about that?"

"Okay," Christian said, still sounding a bit disappointed but pacified by the idea that he would be spending lots of time with his family.

They pulled into the driveway of his sister's high-priced subdivision and stopped at a small house that stood as the security gate.

"Wow," Christian said, pointing at a huge brick house sitting on a hill. "I wanna live in that house."

"That is nice, huh?" Ian said.

"Yeah. Look at that one," Christian said, pointing to another one. "When I get rich, I'ma buy us one."

"That's good to know," Ian said as he handed the security guard his identification. "I'm here to see my sister, Andrea Marion."

"Yes, sir, Mr. DeMarco," the guard, who looked like an old Will Smith, said with a pleasant smile. "Your name is on her guest list. Do you know how to get to her place?"

"Yes," Ian said. "It's been a minute, but I think I remember."

"She's on this street all the way at the end of the cul de sac," he said.

"Thanks," Ian said and pulled off. He felt butterflies in his stomach as he approached his sister's huge stucco home. He saw the long Lincoln Town Car, which meant his father had already arrived. A few other cars were in the driveway, and he pulled up behind one, then killed his ignition and took a deep breath. He looked back at his son, who returned his stare with a big smile.

"Let's go see the family," he said and felt good about his first step back to the way things were.

Chapter 11

"As it stands right now, Ms. Zaire, you haven't been officially charged with any crime," homicide detective Errol Shilo said. Detective Shilo was about five feet ten inches tall, was black as coal and had muscles everywhere. His shiny bald head seemed to glow when he moved a certain way under the florescent ceiling lights. His partner, Detective Lester Sullivan, was the physical opposite. He was tall, Caucasian, rail thin, and had a head full of gray hair.

"However," Detective Sullivan, playing the bad cop in the good cop/bad cop game, said, "you are our prime suspect. There is no doubt about that."

Zola stared at the man as if he would break out laughing and tell her this was all some cruel joke. He returned her glare with a stone face as if he were reading her mind and letting her know this was far from a joke.

"I didn't murder anybody," Zola said as the man's words stung her insides. "And I don't appreciate y'all coming in here accusing me of it either."

"We're not accusing you of anything, Ms. Zaire. We're investigating a crime, and you are a suspect. No more, no less," Detective Shilo said.

"Yet you really don't seem all that bothered by the news that your mother is dead. Why is that? Could it be that you helped send her to the afterlife?" Detective Sullivan asked.

"I didn't send her anywhere," Zola snapped.

"Look at you. You're pretty cold and nonchalant. I know if someone told me my mother was murdered, I'd be a complete wreck," Sullivan said.

"Good for you," she spat.

"So why did you do it?" Detective Sullivan asked.

"Why did I do what?" she asked.

"Why did you murder your mother?"

"Didn't I just tell you I didn't murder anybody? I'm not confessing to a crime just so you lazy bastards can write it off your list of things to do. Screw y'all. Do your investigation."

"What kind of relationship did you have with your mother?" Detective Shilo asked in a soft tone, playing his good-cop role to a T.

"There wasn't a relationship. I didn't like her, and she didn't like me. I hate that someone killed her, but I didn't have anything to do with it. My mother was a bitch, but I would never do anything to her," Zola said.

"So you didn't like your mother?" Sullivan interjected.

"Are you deaf?" she said. "What part of what I just said did you not understand?"

"Why were you guys arguing?" Shilo asked.

"I don't recall us arguing," Zola said.

"Your neighbor," Sullivan said, pausing to flip through his notepad, "Mrs. Ham said she heard you guys yelling at each other. Then she said she saw you rushing from the house. Why were you in such a hurry to leave?"

"She told me to get out," Zola said dryly.

"Do you mind telling us what happened to your face?" Shilo asked.

"I don't recall," Zola said. As the words left her lips, she knew her response sounded like a lie.

"Could that be from the struggle? Could it be that Sara fought you with everything she had, yet you still plunged your knife into her? Not just once, not twice, but thirty-three times? You stuck that knife into your mother over and over and over until she lay dead. That's what happened. Why don't you just admit it? If you confess, maybe we can work with you. If not, then you take the chance of spending the rest of your life in prison."

Zola sighed as if this entire scene were more a nuisance than anything. She tuned the men out and tried to dig deep into her soul to find something that would make her feel bad about her mother's demise, but there was nothing there.

"Hello. Over here," Detective Sullivan said, waving his hand in Zola's face to get her attention.

"What?" she said, shooting the detective a cold stare.

"Why were you over at your mother's house?" Sullivan asked.

"Don't know," Zola said.

"You don't know?" Sullivan said. "Well, you do have the right to remain silent, but I wish you would help us out. I mean, because, as of right now, my thinking is that you're a cold-blooded killer, Ms. Zaire. And I believe you finished the job that you started when you were a little girl."

"Do you even know what really happened when I was a little girl?" Zola said.

"Sure," Detective Sullivan said. "I have it right here in my little pad. It says you tried to stab your mother and her then-boyfriend you were having an affair with."

Zola shook her head as if to say, "Unbelievable."

"Was there anyone else at your mother's house you know of?" Detective Shilo asked.

"No," Zola said. She wouldn't dare mention her brother's name even though she couldn't help but wonder how or if he fit into this whole scenario. He had yet to return her phone calls, which was weird considering he had shown so much concern for her when they had last seen each other. "I don't even know how I got there. I woke up in my old room. She came in there, screaming about how I had to get my stuff together and get out, so I got my bag and left. When I left her house, she was sitting on the sofa watching some television show."

"What show?" Shilo asked. "Do you remember?"

"One of those TV judge shows," Zola said. "*Judge Joe Brown* or *Judge Judy* or something. I can't say for certain."

"So tell me," Detective Sullivan said, "you said you didn't remember how you got to your mother's house. What else don't you remember?"

"Now that has to be the stupidest question I've ever heard. Are you sure you're a detective?" Zola asked.

The officer shot her a look that said, "Don't try me," before he continued. "Let me rephrase the question. Do you think you would remember killing your mother?"

"I think I might remember that," Zola replied sarcastically.

"My investigation tells me, and you confirm it, that there was a great deal of resentment toward your mother. Did all of this start because she broke up the little fling you had going with her man? Then the father of your child mysteriously kills himself. Death seems to follow you wherever you go, Ms. Zaire."

"Rapes," Zola snapped. "Both of them were rapes. One was an outright rape, and the other was statutory. Why are you in here harassing me? Why don't you get out of here and go arrest some of those rapists who prey on young girls instead of sitting here blaming me? Do you know how old I was when I had my son? Huh? Do you know how old his father is? Is that in your li'l pad?"

"If that's the case, then why didn't you ever call the authorities?" Sullivan asked.

"Because most of the authorities are just your stupid ass," Zola said as she felt her temperature rise at the mere thought of what happened to her as a child. "I think it's time I speak to an attorney," Zola said.

"Well," Detective Sullivan said with a smile, "Ms. Zaire, you certainly have a right to an attorney. But you best believe that this is not over. I'm sure we're on the right track, so we will be back."

"Yeah, well, good luck," Zola said. "The fact that I was at my mother's house isn't reason enough for you to charge me with murder, you idiots!"

"Maybe not. But you had motive and opportunity. Add to that that you have a very nasty disposition about you and there might just be enough there," Detective Sullivan said with a wicked smile as if nothing gave him more pleasure than to send a person to one of Georgia's prisons. "You're not under arrest yet, but it's coming. I would suggest you hire a good lawyer."

Zola's heart dropped down to the floor. Even in death, her mother was still causing her pain.

Detective Shilo wore a pained expression on his face as if he didn't agree with the senior detective. He stood and nodded at her as they left the room.

Chapter 12

Ian and Christian stood on the large wraparound porch of his sister's palatial estate and rang the doorbell. Seconds later, the door flew open, and Andrea stood in her large foyer with an even larger smile on her face.

"Well, well, well, look at you guys," Andrea said, reaching down to hug her nephew. "Hi, Christian."

"Hi," he said shyly from his spot hiding behind his father's leg.

"You don't have to hide from me. I'm Auntie Andrea and I loooooove you," she said, drawing a smile from the little boy. "And listen, that fireman's hat is so cool. Are you going to be a fireman when you grow up?"

"Yes," Christian said, smiling but still holding on to Ian's leg.

"Well, that's great," Andrea said, then turned her attention to Ian and gave him a hug. "Hello, stranger. Y'all come on in. Christian, did I tell you that you are one handsome dude?"

"Thank you," Christian said with a wide smile.

Ian smiled too, and once they were inside, he reached out and gave his sister another tight and long-overdue hug. He felt himself getting emotional, so he released his embrace.

"It's okay," Andrea said, wiping away her own tears. Ian's self-imposed exile from the family seemed to hurt her the most. They were always the closest of all the siblings, and when Ian cut the family off, she suffered the most. "I'm so happy to see you two handsome devils. Go on in the living room. The gang's all here."

Ian walked in and immediately felt the nostalgia. It was like one big family reunion. His father was asleep by the fireplace. He had a half-finished beer in one hand and a newspaper in the other. His brother, Malcolm, whom he hadn't seen in years, was holding a remote control and flicking through videos of who was obviously his young son.

"What in the world?" Malcolm said as he dropped the remote and stared at his big brother. He frowned and rushed over to grab the man who was his protector when he was younger, and he placed him in a bear hug. "Man, it's good to see you. And when did this li'l fella get so big? Oh, my God. Hey, Christian."

"Hi," Christian said shyly to the man he could only remember from pictures.

Malcolm was always called the crybaby of the bunch because he was such a sensitive kid. And it seemed that getting older didn't change his emotional state. Tears streamed down his face as he stared at his nephew and big brother, shaking his head as if he were trying to keep his emotions in check.

"Now don't you go crying, Malcolm," Ian said as he rubbed his brother's head just as he did when he was a kid.

"Man, hush." Malcolm nodded toward an Asian woman who was sitting on the sofa. "That's my wife, Ming."

"Wife?" Ian asked. "You found somebody to be willing to spend more than a few hours with you?"

"Shut up, man. I sent you an invitation to the wedding, but your sorry butt didn't even respond. You could've sent a note or something. Anyway, Ming, this is my big brother, Ian. He's the butt wipe I told you about."

Ming, short with long black hair and a baby-doll face, stood and bowed to Ian. "Heard much about you. Good things. No butt wipe stuff," she said with a smile. "Nice to meet you, Ian."

"It's nice to meet you too, Ming. This is my son, Christian."

"Handsome boy," Ming said, reaching out to touch Christian's hand.

Christian smiled politely and shook her hand.

"Such a gentleman," Ming said. "Looks just like a smaller version of his father."

"Man," Malcolm said, butting in, "why didn't you return my calls? You don't do family like that, dude."

"All I can say is I'm sorry," Ian said, holding his hands out to his sides. "And please wipe those tears off your face. You're gonna let your wife see you crying."

Malcolm twisted his lip. "Yeah. She knows I'm sensitive. That's part of my sex appeal. I keep it real. I'm just happy to see you, big bro," Malcolm said, reaching out for another hug.

"Man, move," Ian said, pushing his brother away. "I've been here five minutes, and you've already hugged me five times. Go on back over there and play with your videos."

"Oh, you gonna act like that," Malcolm said, fanning his brother away. "Fine then. I see you still have an attitude problem."

Christian looked around at the roomful of strangers who were all smiling at him. He noticed his grandfather sleeping in the chair. He zeroed in on him and took off running. He stopped, planted, and leaped up on his grandfather's lap.

"Ough," Colin said with a loud grunt. He opened his eyes and frowned. Once his eyes adjusted to the little brown face smiling back at him, he returned a smile of his own. "Christian," he said, "boy, you gonna break one of your granddaddy's bones."

"Hey, Granddaddy," he said. "I got my car with me. You wanna play?"

"Boy, you get right down to business, don'tcha?" Colin said with a smile. He rubbed his grandson's head and lifted him up and placed Christian back down in his chair. "We'll take care of that playing in just a second. Let your granddaddy take a bathroom break."

Colin walked over to Ian. He stopped in front of his son and extended his hand. "Nice to see ya, son."

Ian looked at the hand. Everyone in the room watched, fully aware of the rift between the two men.

"Nice to see you too," Ian said, smiling and pushing away his father's hand. He pulled the old man in for a tight embrace. He held his father for a long time as if he were making up for the years they were separated by circumstance.

"Oh, now you wanna get all mushy. Is this Ian or Malcolm?"

"Why y'all wanna get on me just because I don't hide my feelings?" Malcolm asked.

"Hush, Malcolm," Colin said as his watery eyes told how he really felt. "Let me go to the bathroom, boy. You know I'm not as young as I used to be. That beer got my bladder working overtime. Andrea, you know you're supposed to hide the beer from me when I come over here."

"Do you need me to run out and get you some Depends, Pops?" Ian joked, surprised as anyone else that he picked up his old personality without a hitch.

"I might," Colin said with a chuckle, then made his way to the hallway bathroom.

"I'm so happy you did that," Andrea said. "He really needed that. You know you were always his favorite."

"I thought I was his favorite," Malcolm said, looking serious.

"You are his favorite. Ever since he took you from those crackheads," Ian said with a straight face.

"What crackheads?" Malcolm asked.

Ian put his hand over his mouth. "Oh, Lord, I done said too much."

Malcolm laughed and gave Ian the middle finger.

Andrea laughed too. "I am so happy to have everyone here. This is the best. You know, Ian, it just about killed him when you shut him out. He won't admit it, but he's probably in that bathroom crying his eyes out."

"Yeah," Ian said as he felt his own eyes get a little watery. "I don't know what I was thinking. I just couldn't get that night out of my head, and I blamed . . . Well, there is nothing I can do about it. It's time to move on."

"So true. Now that you are back, I need a favor," Andrea said as the smile on her face disappeared and was replaced by a worried look.

"What?"

"I need you to talk to your nephew. He's about lost his everlasting mind. Wants to be a thug. For what? I don't know. I have taken him to tour the jails, sent him to etiquette classes, put him on punishment until he was blue in the face, but nothing seems to work. I sent him to live with his father, but—"

"Wait a minute. What do you mean you sent him to live with his father? When did you guys split up?" Ian asked.

"About two years ago," Andrea said, shaking her head.

"Damn," Ian said. "Are you for real?"

"Yes, Ian. Life went on while you stopped living. But anyway, that sorry thing sent him right back to me. Talking about he won't listen to him. Duh! That's why I sent him to live with you in the first place, nut. Anyway, if you will talk to him before you leave, I would greatly appreciate it."

"What happened with you and Kenny if you don't mind me asking?"

"No, I don't mind at all. It's pretty simple actually. I caught him having an affair with a man. And that man just happened to be my boss. So I got fired, I sued his tail and settled out of court for a nice sum of money, and now they are living in Florida."

"Are you serious?" Ian said. "Wow."

"I wish I were lying," Andrea said, shaking her head. Ian could tell the thought still pained her.

"This is Atlanta," Malcolm chimed in. "That's why I moved. I got tired of dudes looking at me crazy. I was at a movie one day and got a li'l teary-eyed over a scene, and this big, buff dude gonna hand me a tissue and touch my leg, talking 'bout he understands. I was like hell nah. Packed my bags that night and moved. Damn that."

"Shut up, Malcolm," Ian said.

"I'm just saying. I don't get down like that," Malcolm said.

"Are you okay, Andrea?" Ian asked.

"I don't have a choice. He claimed he just couldn't live a lie anymore. So I guess he and his new man are over there living the truth. And I know KJ's behavior is a direct result of that."

"How old is KJ now?"

"He's thirteen."

"That's a tough age anyway without having to deal with finding out that your dad is gay. Where is he?" Ian asked.

"At a friend's house playing Xbox. That's where he spends most of his time. He's also suspended from school for having marijuana in his locker. Then he had the audacity to kick the drug dog," Andrea said.

"Damn," Ian said. "I'll be sure to talk to him, but for one thing, he's not on vacation, so why are you letting him play video games?"

"I can't monitor that boy twenty-four seven, so if he's gonna sneak and play it when I'm not home, I might as well not even fool myself," Andrea said.

Ian took a deep breath and nodded. He didn't realize how much he had dropped the ball on his responsibility to his family.

Colin walked out of the bathroom and motioned for Ian to come and join him on the deck.

"Granddaddy," Christian said, holding up his car as his sign that he was ready to play.

"Let me talk to your dad for a second and I will be all yours, okay? But in the meantime, why don't you show your uncle Malcolm what you have?" Colin said.

"Okay," Christian said.

"Whatcha got there, fireman?" Malcolm said, walking over to his nephew.

Ian and his father walked out on the spacious deck and enjoyed the view of a large man-made lake equipped with a water fountain in the middle of it. About twenty-five ducks were swimming, and every few minutes a fish would splash in the water. Colin lit up a Cuban cigar and offered one to his son. Ian declined.

"I'm happy to see you, son," Colin said as he pulled on the cigar. "You seem like you're getting back to your old self. Joking with your old man, smiling and stuff."

"Yeah," Ian said, nodding his head. "I'm glad Andrea invited me over. It feels so good to be around family again. It's time to move on. I don't know what took me so long."

"We all have our own process, son," Colin said. "Trust me on that one. I still . . . well, anyway, I'm just happy that you seem to be happy, and that's all that matters."

"You're looking good, Pops. I see you've been taking care of yourself."

"Thanks. The doctor took me off that pork. Hurt my feelings something awful, too, son. I swear I almost cried like Malcolm. Oh, what I wouldn't give for two smothered pork chops, a side of collard greens cooked with a big piece of fatback, and some macaroni with cheese." Colin closed his eyes and appeared to savor the taste of what was now a forbidden meal.

Ian chuckled. "You don't need it. Soul food is too high in sodium and cholesterol. That's why black people are always dying off so early."

"Yeah, but everything they allow me to eat tastes like shit," Colin said, shaking his head. "The man even took ice cream from me. How can ice cream be bad for you? I drew the line right there. I eat it anyway. Rocky Road with the marshmallows in it, or butter pecan. My God. I figure if I'm gonna die, then I'll be happy. I hope they find me with half a gallon of butter pecan in my stomach."

Ian laughed. He didn't realize how much he missed his father's sense of humor. "Man, you're crazy," Ian said.

"Yeah," Colin said, taking a drag from his Cuban cigar.

"Dad," Ian said, "I saw something on the news about that lady I helped out. I think she's in jail."

"Jail?"

"Yeah," Ian said. "They said something about her murdering her mother, but something about that story doesn't seem possible. At least, not the way they described it. The newscaster said the mother was stabbed to death, but I can't see that. The woman I dropped off could barely walk."

Colin scratched his temple, a true sign he was in deep thought, and then nodded his head. "Why are you so interested in helping this woman? Didn't you tell me that you didn't know her?"

"I don't know her," Ian said. "I never met her before the day I helped her, but something has me wanting to make sure she's okay. And I know it's going to eat me up until I find out what's going on."

"Yeah," Colin said. "I understand that. That's a DeMarco trait. Sometimes we can't leave well enough alone. I sent a couple of guys over to her place to snoop around. The guy who beat her up isn't dead."

"Yeah, I know," Ian said. "I saw him. I was on my route, and he came running out of his house with his trash. Didn't seem to recognize me at all. No cuts, no bruises, or anything from where I hit him. I saw his face split open with my own two eyes. There was blood all over the place, and now nothing? I don't understand that one. I kept his trash and went through it. There were all kinds of dried-up bloody bandages in there, but his face didn't show any signs of that beatdown."

"You said he was running?" Colin asked.

"Yep. He flagged us down because we had already passed his house."

"That's interesting. I need to have a conversation with the guys I sent over there. I was told that his legs were broken. Are you sure it was the same guy?"

"I'm one hundred percent sure," Ian said.

"Okay," Colin said, calm as ever. "I'll look into it."

"Thanks. Did Andrea talk to you about KJ?" Ian asked.

"Nah," he said. "But I kind of figured something was going on with him. He's a teenager, and she's now a single mother. Sometimes that can be a recipe for disaster. What did she tell you?"

"She said he's lost his mind. Doing some crazy things. Got caught with some weed at school and has been acting out."

Colin frowned. "Well, you talk to him and keep me posted. It's got to be tough in today's society when your daddy turns gay on you, but it's amplified when that dummy gets on television and talks about how gays should be allowed to get married."

"He was on TV?" Ian asked. "I would've never suspected Kenny to be gay."

"He's one of them down-low fellas. Or, at least, he was. I have more respect for the ones who walk around switching than for them closet punks. That's why the disease rate is so high. Sleeping with a man but then wanna run around and jump in bed with a woman because they are too weak to be who they are. If you gay, then just be gay. You don't have to walk around wearing dresses, but don't lie to people or yourself."

"Yeah," Ian said, nodding in agreement. "What television show was he on?"

"I don't know. I can't keep up with that stuff. He just didn't think about his son and how his coming out would affect him. But this is a different day, son," Colin said.

Ian looked out as the daylight turned to dusk, and he noticed that the ducks had gone on their way.

"Dinner's ready, guys," Andrea's voice said, but she was nowhere to be seen.

"Oh. She can't come out here and tell us. She has to show off the intercom, huh?" Ian said with a smile. "This place is off the chain."

"Yeah. It's nice. And I'm starving," Colin said. "Let's go eat."

Chapter 13

Ravon hadn't been out of prison for a full week, yet he was on the run. He wasn't sure where he was going, but he had to leave. He rushed around the apartment throwing all of his clothes and belongings into a big Hefty trash bag and rushed around his girlfriend's apartment looking for anything he might need for his new life far away from the state of Georgia. Sweat was pouring from his pores even though the temperature outside was below thirty degrees. He paused and calmed himself. He looked at his woman, who was sitting on the sofa, rocking back and forth. Lisa was a very pretty woman. She was naturally large, and she wore it well. Her creamy-colored skin was flushed from crying. They had waited five long years to be together, and now they were about to be separated again.

"I didn't know what else to do!" Ravon said after he shared every single detail of what had happened at his mother's house and how he wished he never took the phone call. "I didn't have a choice. It was him or me. I really didn't have a choice."

"I know, so why don't you just call the police and tell them what happened?" Lisa pleaded through the stream of tears running down her chubby cheeks.

"Lisa, you know I can't do that. They will lock me up first, then ask questions later. I just left prison. I'm guilty until proven innocent in their eyes."

"But the key word is that you're innocent. So let them prove you innocent. I have some money saved. We can get a lawyer," she said.

"Even if they find me innocent, I still had a gun. They will try to send me back to prison for that alone. I just can't take the chance," Ravon said.

"I knew you shouldn't have gone over there. I could feel that something wasn't right," Lisa said.

"Yeah, I had that feeling too," Ravon said, shaking his head in disbelief of the situation he found himself in. "I should've stayed my ass right here. I can't go back to prison, Lisa. I can't even take the chance."

"Where are you going?" she asked.

"I don't know," Ravon said. "I can't believe this is happening to me. I must be cursed or something. Damn."

"No, you're not cursed. I am. I finally find a man who treats me good, and this happens. I wanna go with you, Ray."

"If things cool down, I'll send for you," Ravon said. "I hope that nosy-ass lady next door didn't see me."

Ravon walked over to his woman. He hugged her as tight as he could before pulling himself away.

"Is your car going to make it on a highway?" Lisa asked, referring to the hooptie he had just purchased.

"We'll see," he said and gave her one last kiss before walking toward the front door.

"Ray, wait," Lisa said, nervously rubbing her hands together. "How am I going to get in touch with you?"

"I don't know. I'll get my hands on another cell phone and call you."

"No," she said and ran to the bedroom and returned with her cell phone. "Take this. I'll get a new one tomorrow. I need to be able to reach you."

"A'ight, thanks."

"I love you, Ray."

"I love you too," he said and reached out to wipe away her tears.

"I wish you could stay!" she said, stalling for more time.

"Me too, but listen, if the police come by here, you tell them I've been out of town looking for work for a few days."

"Okay," she said.

He turned around and gave her one more look. He placed his hand to his mouth and blew her a kiss before walking out of the apartment. He hustled down the stairs with his belongings slung across his shoulders. Before walking into the parking lot, he scanned the area for police, and once the coast was clear, he ran over to his jalopy and got in. He turned the ignition, and the hooptie came to life. He couldn't help but relive how peaceful his life was just a few short hours ago.

Ravon lay on his back, smoking a Phillies Blunt cigar with the tobacco replaced with a different herb of marijuana that had a purplish hue. The potent weed was imported from the streets of Los Angeles and known there as the "sticky icky." He had always loved the way weed smoke made him feel. His troubles were a thing of the past as long as he had some weed in his system, and as the potent Los Angeles "sticky icky" was inhaled into his lungs, the world was a beautiful place.

Lisa was lying beside him, totally unconscious and snoring for the entire neighborhood to hear. Sleep always stole her away after their sex sessions. He looked at her and smiled as if his penis were the reason she was totally exhausted. "Yeah," he said, "don't you go to war with the big dog, girl. Look atcha. Knocked the hell out," he said as he took another puff.

Ravon and Lisa shared a small two-bedroom apartment in a middle-class neighborhood in Stone Mountain with her son, Devin. Devin was away for the weekend with his father, so they had the apartment all to themselves.

Ravon took a deep pull from the blunt and held it in his lungs until he coughed. He couldn't understand how something that felt so good could cause such violent convulsions within his body. With every puff he felt as if he were about to lose a lung. He threw his legs over the edge of the bed, stood up, and stretched. His head was a little woozy from the weed, but his stomach was begging to be fed.

He walked into the kitchen, reached into the cabinet, and grabbed a box of Frosted Flakes and a big Tupperware container. He emptied half the box of cereal into the bowl. He opened the refrigerator and pulled out a gallon of milk and covered the flakes. A big smile creased his face when he thought about all those nights in jail when he wished he could do something as simple as get up and walk into another room. Now he was free, and he couldn't help but savor the moment.

He replaced the milk and the box of cereal, grabbed his bowl, and opened the sliding door to the balcony. He walked outside and took in the night air. If someone had walked by at that moment, they would have thought he was plumb crazy. Here he was sitting on the balcony at two in the morning, in the winter, wearing nothing but his birthday suit and eating a bowl of cereal. If prison taught him anything, it was to never take life for granted.

He had promised himself that, once he was free, he would enjoy the little things. Things like taking a walk in the park. People who lived in the hood never took advantage of nature. He had been living in Atlanta all his life and never once visited the King Center, Stone Mountain Park, Sweet Auburn Avenue, Ebenezer Baptist Church, or any of the other historical places the city had to offer. He had spent his entire life confined to a small area of the city all because he never opened himself up to think outside his comfort zone. But that was all about to change.

The apartment phone rang, and he jumped to get it before it woke Lisa up. He placed his bowl on the counter and answered the phone. "Hello," he said, wondering who could be calling the house at this time of morning.

"Ravon," Sara said, "this ya momma. I need for you to get over here. These li'l bad-ass kids out there selling drugs on my front porch. Now I know they dumb, but I didn't know the li'l fuckers were crazy. I told them I was gonna call the police, and they ran off, but now they're back. I went outside with my gun, and all they did was show me theirs. I'm tired of these li'l bastards. They making all kind of noise, and I can't get no damn sleep."

"Call the police," he said.

"And play that li'l game all night? The police are full of shit. I ain't fooling with them. You coming or not?"

Ravon sighed. He was really enjoying his high and really didn't feel like dealing with his mother or the brats who were giving her problems, but he'd promised himself while sitting in prison that he would look after the woman.

"Hello?" Sara said.

"Yeah, I'm here. I'll be over there in a minute."

"You better hurry up because my patience is running out. I don't wanna have to shoot one of these li'l niggas."

"Don't do that," Ravon said, stomping his foot with frustration. "I'm on my way."

"Yeah, well . . . Where is your cell phone? I've been calling you for two days. Good thing I remembered that I wrote Lisa's number down on the calendar."

"I lost it."

"Lost it? Damn, boy, you would forget your head if it weren't attached to your neck."

"Have you talked to Zola?"

"Hell no. For what?"

"'Cause she's your daughter."

"No, she ain't no daughter of mine. I can do without her ass. She's still running around here feeling sorry for herself and blaming me for everything that's wrong in her life."

"And so you're just going to . . . well, whatever," Ravon said, deciding against trying to salvage a relationship that was forever broken.

"How did you lose your damn phone?"

"You want me to come over or are you gonna keep asking me questions?" Ravon asked.

Something cracked in his ear as his mother slammed her end of the phone down as if that should be a good enough answer. He shook his head at the nutcase he had for a mother and placed the phone back on its base. After grabbing his bowl of cereal, he walked into the living room and sat on the sofa to finish feeding his munchies. Ravon grabbed the remote control and flipped through the channels. The video channels were all filled with infomercials, so he flipped through the rotation again.

"Seven hundred channels and not a damn thing worth watching," he said to himself. "Damn, I wish I hadn't answered that phone. Just my luck I get over there and have to shoot one of those li'l fools."

History told him that any confrontation with youngsters this time of morning could easily turn violent. And that could lead him right back to prison or to death. He picked up the phone and dialed 911.

"Nine one one. What is your emergency?"

"I'd like to report a trespasser at my mother's house," Ravon said.

"Will you hold please?" the operator said.

Ravon frowned but held the line. After being in that same position for four minutes, he pulled the phone away from his ear and looked at it. "Hello? Damn. This is a joke. What kind of emergency line is this?"

After hanging up on 911, Ravon stood and wondered why he was going to go over to Sara's house to check on her. He didn't really care about her because she wouldn't allow you to care about her. But she was still his mother. Something inside of him was telling him to stay away, but he brushed the thought away and walked back into the bedroom and got dressed.

He put on some underwear, a pair of Levi jeans, and a sweatshirt, and he slipped his size-twelve feet into his trusty Timberland boots. He grabbed the car keys and leaned down and kissed Lisa on her forehead. He stood and stared at his woman. Physically she wasn't his type, but she was good as gold. And the way she stood by him when he was incarcerated placed her at the top of his list.

Lisa was a few pounds overweight, her skin was almost white, and she was as ghetto as the next chick. The thing that separated Lisa from the other hood girls was that she wanted a better life for herself and her son. And even more important, she was willing to put in the work to get there. She had just enrolled in night classes to earn her associate degree from Georgia's Perimeter College and was trying to get Ravon to do the same. His superficial side hated to admit it, but he loved her.

Lisa stirred and looked at him with sleepy eyes. "Where are you going, Ray?"

"I need to run by Sara's house. Some kids are out there bothering her, and I need to go talk to them. I called the police, but those bastards put me on hold and never came back to the phone."

"Oh, okay," she said and rolled back over. "Be careful."

"Will do," he said. He grabbed his coat and the keys for her car. He had just purchased a little Saturn for himself, but it was in dire need of a muffler. Whenever he drove it, everyone within a five-mile radius could hear him coming.

Ravon got into Lisa's Honda and headed toward his mother's house, which was only about a ten-minute drive from where he was. He backed out of the parking lot and had this sinking feeling in his gut. Something wasn't right. He made a few turns here and there, and before long he was turning onto the street where his mother lived.

Ravon drove slowly as he scanned the streets looking for signs of trouble. As he eased past Sara's house, he checked out the front porch but didn't see any kids. He drove down to the end of the street, then turned around in someone's driveway. Coming back up the street, he slowly pulled into an empty spot in front of Sara's house. He stared at the house before he got out of the car, then walked up the driveway and stopped. Was he imagining that he saw the curtain in the living room open then close?

Ravon's gut was screaming at him to get out of there, so he turned back around and went to the car. He opened the driver-side door, leaned inside, and felt up under the seat until his fingers touched the cold steel of the .38-caliber handgun. He gripped it, slipped it in his pocket, and closed the car door, then turned back around and walked up the driveway and climbed the stairs to the old white house.

He knocked on the door, but nobody answered. He knocked harder, but there was only silence on the other side. He scratched his head and walked over to see if he could see inside the house. The television was on, and *he thought he saw Sara lying on the sofa. He knocked on the window, but she didn't move.*

Did he just see somebody's shadow in the kitchen area?

He pulled his gun out and jumped off the porch. Something wasn't right, and he could feel it as he made his way around the side of the house to the back door. Ravon eased up the back steps and tried the doorknob. He turned it, and much to his surprise, it opened. His heartbeat was racing so fast that he thought a cardiac arrest was on the horizon. His pistol was already in his hand, so he chambered a round into his gun and placed it in front of him. As he stepped inside the kitchen, his instincts kicked in just in time.

Pow. A gunshot blasted into the door behind him, sending wood fragments and splinters everywhere.

Ravon jumped down onto the floor and stuck his gun around the wall and let off two shots from his own gun. He only had six bullets, so he made sure to keep that in mind. He stayed low and waited for whoever it was to return fire. He heard a man groan and make a sound he'd never heard before. Down on his stomach, he crawled very slowly, almost snaillike, until he could see in the direction where he sent his bullets. He looked to his right and saw the bottom of two black boots. A white man was lying down on the floor clutching his chest.

Pow! Ravon's gunshot blast shook the calm of the night as he shot one more time into the man's body. He wasn't sure if he was dead or if he was trying to lure him in. The white man's body shook, and he grabbed his shoulder with his left hand, but he didn't take his right one from his chest. Ravon jumped up after seeing that the man wasn't a threat anymore, and he walked over to him.

"Who the hell are you?" he asked the man, who was now bleeding from his mouth, chest, and shoulder.

The man didn't respond. He couldn't respond if he wanted to. His eyes were fluttering, and his mouth was opening and closing as he gasped through the flowing blood for air.

Ravon looked at him and could tell right away that the man had done prison time. Tattoos were all over the place, even on his face and neck. His long, stringy hair was pulled back into a ponytail.

Ravon looked down and saw the man's gun a few feet away from him. He thought about picking it up but didn't want his fingerprints on it, so he kicked it away. He took a few steps toward the living room and could see his mother. Sara was covered in blood and not moving. He called her name as he eased over to her. As he got closer, he could see her eyes were wide open, but there was no life there. Ravon looked around and decided it was time to get out of the house. He was a convicted felon who had just shot a man—a white man at that. In the state of Georgia, that was enough to get you death by lethal injection. Never mind the fact that this man was in his mother's house, she was dead, and he had taken a shot at him. None of that would matter in a court of law.

Ravon took a deep breath and hustled back through the kitchen. He glanced over at the man he had just shot. The man was still grimacing in pain and holding his wounds. His mouth was wide open as he gasped for air, but he was losing the battle to stay alive. He looked up at Ravon with pleading eyes.

"Help," the man managed to say.

Ravon did a double take and was amazed at the man's arrogance. "You just killed my mother and tried to kill me, yet you think I'm going to help you stay alive?"

There would be no help coming. The man had seen his face, and he wasn't going back to prison for anybody, especially for a man like the one lying on the dirty kitchen floor. Ravon turned his gun on the man and fired another shot into the man's midsection, which stopped the pleading and the gasping and the life. The man let out a gargling sound, then closed his eyes for good.

Ravon ran and checked all the bedrooms to make sure nobody else was in the house, and once he knew he was alone, he ran out through the back door. He hustled to the Honda and jumped inside. He took a deep breath and calmly turned the ignition and eased away from his mother's house, being careful not to speed.

Chapter 14

Zola stared at the television set that was mounted on the wall near the window of her hospital room. She couldn't believe what she was seeing. Her picture was being plastered all over the evening news as a prime suspect in the death of her mother. God knew that she hated Sara with every ounce of her being, but she could never kill her. It just wasn't in her nature. She thought about the many times when she almost fell down while jogging just to avoid stepping on an ant or some other insect, and now she was being plastered on Fox 5 News as a lead person of interest in a murder of a real live person.

There was a knock on the door, and Zola pulled her nightgown up a little closer to her neck. "Come in," she said.

Kecia walked in, followed by a woman with closely cropped hair and a very light complexion. The woman had a pleasant smile and looked very familiar to her.

"Hi there," Kecia said with a wide smile as if she had just hit the lottery or something. "I really hate to just show up like this with a visitor, but whatever."

"How did you guys get in? Visiting hours are over," Zola said.

"Girl, please. I'm from New York," Kecia said. "I told them I was your family, I came all the way from California, and I have a plane to catch in the morning."

"You're a mess, but you are family," Zola said. "The only sister I have."

"That's right," Kecia said. "Anyway, this is my god-mother, Pearl. Pearl Cleage."

"Hi." Zola smiled as she connected the name with the face. She had just read one of Ms. Cleage's books a few months ago when she heard about how good it was on Oprah Winfrey's website. "I love your work."

"Thank you," Pearl said with a soothing, velvety voice. "I hope you don't mind me showing up like this."

"Oh, no. Not at all," Zola said. "I'm a huge fan. It's a pleasure to meet you."

Pearl smiled and nodded her appreciation. "I under-stand you're in a bit of a bind. I want to help."

"Being in a bind is the story of my life, Ms. Cleage," Zola said. "I have no idea how I'm the so-called prime suspect because I had nothing to do with killing my mother."

"They are just sweating you," Kecia said. "Fishing for anything they can use against you."

"If that's the case, then why is my picture on television?" Zola asked. "When I left her house, she was sitting on the sofa watching television."

"I hear that you and your mother weren't close," Pearl said.

"No. I didn't like her, and she didn't like me," Zola said.

Pearl frowned and shook her head as if she was think-ing this was a story she had heard too many times before. Then she walked closer to the bed and ran her hand across Zola's face, smoothing her hair back into place.

"It has to be illegal for them to do that to me, right? I wish I could afford an attorney to sue them," Zola said, fighting a losing battle with her tears. She had had to be strong for so long, but there was something about being in the room with these two women that made her let down her guard. There was something special, almost angelic about the lady standing over her, smiling. Pearl's eyes and soft touch told Zola that she could let go of all the pain, frustration, and pent-up rage because now there was a soft place to land. In less than a minute of knowing the woman, she trusted her with everything she had.

What is that all about? she wondered.

"It's okay," Pearl said, embracing Zola's hand with both of hers and seemingly reading her mind. "We will get through this together. I know it's hard, but you are not alone."

"Pearl has a friend who is a very good attorney, and she is already downtown talking to the powers that be on your behalf," Kecia said.

"That's right, so your picture won't be shown anymore," Pearl said.

"I called her the minute I left here when the police showed up. I've been interning downtown with the public defender's office, and I'm well aware of how they do things. It's a shame that the name of the game is clearing the books at any cost. We are not going to let them frame you. I hope you don't mind, but I told Pearl everything that you told me about your past."

Zola nodded but didn't respond.

"The attorney's name is Sharon Capers, and she's very good. One of the best in the business," Pearl said.

"I don't have the money right now," Zola said. "I will have to move a few things around. I have a three-hundred-thousand-dollar loft that I made sure was in my name and a hundred-thousand-dollar car but no money, but I will sell whatever—"

"No, ma'am," Pearl said, shaking her head. "This is not about money. The only thing we want from you is for you to get better. And once this is all behind you, you'll help someone else. Pretty simple, huh?"

Zola nodded. "I don't know what to say."

"There is nothing that needs to be said," Pearl said. "But listen, I really need to get home. My husband and I are going on a little vacation in the morning, but you are in very capable hands. I will be checking on you, okay?"

"Okay," Zola said. "I hope you have fun on your trip."

"Thank you," Pearl said, leaning down and kissing Zola on her forehead. "You get yourself back strong and healthy, and once you are out of here, I would love to have you over for dinner."

"I would love that," Zola said, nodding her head. "Thank you so much for everything."

"Don't mention it," Pearl said. "Kecia, I'll see you later, girl."

"Okay," Kecia said and walked over and gave Pearl a hug before she left. She walked over and sat down beside Zola. "You know, your place is so comfortable. I appreciate you letting me stay there."

"No problem," Zola said. "It's the least I could do."

Zola couldn't stop the tears from running down her face. For all her childhood, she wanted a sister and a real mom, and that had eluded her. Now she wasn't sure how to take this total stranger being nice to her. But the fact that this woman had already set the wheels in motion to get the police off her back placed her on the top of her list.

There was another knock on the door, and in walked a tall white man who was a dead ringer for an older Brad Pitt. Chad Benjamin walked in a few seconds after Pearl had walked out. He nodded at the two ladies as he entered the room. Kecia paused and asked Zola with her eyes if the man was friend or foe. Zola nodded that he was okay.

"Hi there," Chad said to Zola.

"Hi, Chad," Zola said, looking behind him. "How are you? Where is Jason?"

Chad didn't respond.

"Is everything okay?" Zola said, assuming the look on his face was bad news about her son.

"Yes. Everything is fine. Jason is doing great," Chad said.

"Kecia," Zola said. "This is Chad Benjamin. He's my son's . . ." she said, not sure what to call the man.

"Nice to meet you, Chad," Kecia said, reaching out her hand.

"It's nice to meet you too," Chad said with a pleasant smile as he shook Kecia's hand.

"Well, I'll let you guys talk," Kecia said. "Zola, I'll be back to check up on you tomorrow. I put my number on the pad by the phone, so call me if you need anything. I love you, girl."

"I love you too. Be careful out there," Zola said and waited for Kecia to leave.

"I will. Bye. Bye, Chad," Kecia said as she hustled out the door.

Chad nodded to her and looked down at Zola with a concerned expression on his face.

"Have a seat. What's up?" Zola said as she pointed at the chair by the window.

"What's going on with you, Zola? Do you need anything?"

"What do you mean?"

"I was watching the news and—"

"I didn't have anything to do with that," Zola said. "That is my mother, and we weren't the best of friends, but I would never do what those people are saying."

"I believe you, but the problem is . . . well, I won't beat around the bush. Jason saw it and he's quite upset."

"What?" Zola said as her heart hit the floor.

"I tried to keep him away from it, and I did for the six o'clock news, but somehow my wife found a way to let him see it on the seven o'clock broadcast. He's torn up about it."

Zola's tears came back. "Oh, my God," she cried. "I'm totally innocent. I don't want Jason thinking his mother is a murderer. I didn't do anything."

Chad stood and walked over to her. He reached out and touched her hand and gave it a comforting squeeze. "I believe you," he said. "Have you gotten an attorney?"

"Why did she let him see that?" Zola said, feeling her anger rise. She could strangle that woman for trying to poison her son's mind with those shady police officers' lies.

"I don't know, but you can best believe that it caused a huge argument. I'm not sure what her motivation was behind that, but she was wrong," Chad said. "I'm sorry that it happened."

"I wanna talk to Jason," Zola said.

Chad whipped out his cell phone and pushed a button. "Where is Jason?" he said, not bothering with a greeting. "Well, wake him up. Never mind where I am. Just go and get Jason. Carmen, I'm not getting into this with you. Now will you go and get Jason, or should I come home and get him myself?"

Chad sat down and looked at the floor while he waited. He frowned after being placed on hold for a little too long. "This woman," he said, shaking his head.

Zola's heart ached at the thought of her child seeing her picture being attached to the word "murder." Her son's opinion of her was the most important thing in the world. Over the last year she had been privately planning a strategy to get Jason back under her care, but now there was a sense of urgency like never before. She liked Chad, and she used to like his wife. At least, she did until she decided to poison her son's mind against her. Now she knew it was time he came home. The Benjamins had taken care of Jason when she couldn't, and she appreciated that. They had exposed him to people, places, and situations she could only dream about, but they couldn't love him like she could. And now this latest stunt by Carmen was even more motivation to get her life together and prove to the world that she was somebody.

"She hung up," Chad said, taking the phone away from his ear and looking at the screen saver. "I can't believe she hung up. What is wrong with that woman?"

"Don't worry about it," Zola said with a steely determination. "I'll take care of it."

"I just wanted to make sure you were okay," he said, standing. "I will have Jason call you once I get home. Keep your cell phone on."

"He'll have to call the room. I don't have my cell phone with me. I'm not supposed to use it in here."

"Will do," Chad said, walking over and getting the number from the phone on the nightstand.

Chapter 15

Ian looked at his watch. It was almost one o'clock in the morning. Christian was fast asleep on the sofa. His father had already left, and he and Malcolm were sitting on the deck enjoying the night. They lit the fire to keep warm and played catch-up. Ian filled him in with how stagnant his life had been since he lost his wife and daughter, and Malcolm filled him in on his life out west.

"I guess I need to get out of here, man," Ian said as he removed his feet from the patio ottoman. "I'm enjoying the scene too much. Gotta get back to the ghetto."

"There were too many sacrifices made for you to be living in the ghetto," Malcolm said. "I don't want my nephew caught up in some hood crossfire. Then I'm really gonna cry."

"Yeah," Ian said as he turned down the heat on the firepit. "I'm way ahead of ya, li'l bro. That's been on my mind heavy lately. Before we came over here, the natives were outside shooting."

"Come on, Ian," Malcolm said. "If not for yourself, do it for Christian."

Ian nodded. "So when are you headed back to the West Coast?"

"I need to be back on Monday morning. I'm starting a new job at the University of Washington as a career counselor. We fly out Sunday night. I love flying at night, man."

"Oh, yeah? You have a lovely family, bro. I'm proud of you. Got you an Asian woman, huh? She's a gem. I like her."

"Yeah, man. She plays that Asian shit, but her ass was raised in Tacoma, and she got some ghetto ways. Her Kool-Aid is sweeter than a mother. I think she puts about three cups of sugar in a gallon, bro. And she will cuss. Oh, Lord. She gets mad and starts mixing that Asian and hood talk together so much. It's bad, bro. 'You mudda fucka ass licky stupid dick basard,'" Malcolm said with a chuckle. "You don't believe me? I'ma piss her off before we leave so you can hear how she acts."

"Man," Ian said, laughing, "you're crazy. Leave Ming alone."

"Leave Ming alone? She needs to leave me alone. You know I can't beat her, right? Hell, I met her in a karate class. She was my instructor. But you know what I told her? 'You gotta sleep sometime,'" Malcolm said with a straight face.

"Man, I am not messing with you. You are a complete nut," Ian said as he placed the top on the firepit. "I gotta get this boy up so we can get out of here."

"Ian, let him spend the night," Malcolm pleaded. "I wanna spend some time with him. Maybe I can take him to the arcade or something in the morning. He's been asking everybody if he could spend the night. The boy is tired of yo' ass."

Ian chuckled. "Let me talk to Andrea."

"Whatchu think she gonna say, no?"

"Just being courteous, man," Ian said.

Andrea was sitting in a chair across from the fireplace watching television. "Y'all finally decided to come in the house?" she asked.

"Yeah," Ian said. "It's about time we get out of here."

"'We'?" Malcolm said. "How about you just take your butt on and leave my nephew here?"

"Yeah, Ian. He wants to stay," Andrea said. "Let him sleep."

Ian walked over to Christian, who was snoring on the sofa. Ian gave his son a gentle nudge to wake him, and Christian looked up.

"Hi, Daddy," he said, sitting up and rubbing his eyes. "Can I spend the night?"

Ian sighed. "I guess so," he said.

Christian smiled, but he was too tired to do much else, so he laid his head back down on the sofa and drifted back off to sleep.

This would be the first time Ian had ever spent a night without his child, but it wasn't fair to keep treading on the path he had been on. Christian didn't just belong to him. He belonged to his entire family.

The side door leading to the garage opened, and KJ walked in. "What's up, Uncle Malcolm?" he said in his deep teenage voice a few seconds after walking into the living room.

"What's up?" Malcolm said, looking at his watch. "That damn sun gonna be up in a minute. Where you been?"

"Next door," KJ said, then turned his attention to Ian. "Ohhhh, snap. What's up, Uncle Ian? I haven't seen you in ages."

"How you doing, KJ?" Ian said, walking over to give his nephew, who was almost six feet tall, a frat-brother-like hug. "I can't believe how big you've gotten. Are you playing sports?"

"Football and baseball," KJ said.

"When he's not suspended from school," Andrea said.

"Aww, Mom," KJ complained with a frown. "I haven't seen Uncle Ian in I don't know how long, and you gotta start fussing. Don't nobody wanna hear all that."

KJ was the spitting image of his father with a little dose of Andrea thrown in around the lips and cheeks. He was as dark as a Hershey's bar and had a head full of hair, which was twisted up into little dreadlocks.

"I'm glad I waited around, or I would've missed you," Ian said.

"Yeah," KJ said. "I was just two doors down at my friend's house. Is that Christian over there?" he asked, walking over to his little cousin.

"Yep," Ian said, "that's him."

"Boy, he's getting big," KJ said.

"Yeah," Ian said, "and so are you. How tall are you?"

"I don't know," KJ said. "Five eleven, maybe six feet. Something like that."

"I'm going to bed," Malcolm said. He reached out to Ian and gave him his fifteenth hug of the night, and then he turned to KJ and punched him in the chest. "Whatcha gon' do? Huh? Buck up? I'll knock the taste outta ya mouth."

KJ grabbed the spot where he was hit and smiled. "Uncle Malcolm is crazy."

Even after all that he had heard about his nephew, Ian couldn't help but be proud of the young man he was looking at. That was, until he took a closer look at KJ's eyes.

"Are you about to leave?" KJ asked.

"Yeah, man," Ian said, zeroing in on the bloodshot eyes, which was a sure sign of drugs. "I've been here for hours. I called your cell. Why didn't you answer your phone?"

"It's dead. I forgot to charge the thing last night."

"Is that right? Well, listen to me, nephew. I need a favor, KJ."

"Sure," he said. "Anything for you, Uncle Ian."

"I need you to help me move some things at my house. Why don't you grab a change of clothes and ride with me?"

KJ paused. Ian could see that the boy knew something was up.

"I can ask my mom to bring me over in the morning. I'm a little tired," KJ said in a futile attempt to stay home and out of his uncle's tough glare.

Andrea cut in. "I'll tell you right now the answer is no. You can go right now while you have a ride. And you can stay over there for all I care."

KJ dropped his head.

Andrea leaned down and picked Christian up. "Ian, call me tomorrow. If you need me to pack up all his stuff, just say the word."

"Andrea," Ian said, shaking his head, "don't do that."

"I'm just fed up with this boy," Andrea said. "I swear I am. He's been screwing up time after time, and I'm just tired of it."

"Well, you can be fed up, but keep it to yourself," Ian said.

"See how she is? Always putting me down. If you don't want me here, then I'll leave," KJ said.

"And go where?" Andrea said. "Your daddy doesn't want you. He's with who he wants to be with—a damn man."

"Andrea," Ian snapped at his sister. "What's wrong with you? Have you lost your mind? Why would you say something like that?"

"Because it's the damn truth. And every time I get on his case for being a screwup, he claims he's going to leave. Well, leave, KJ. I don't give a damn. As a matter of fact, get out."

"Are you the parent or the child?" Ian snapped.

"Whatever. He can go live with his faggot father," Andrea said as she huffed and puffed. After adjusting Christian on her hip, she walked out of the living room toward her bedroom.

"Uncle Ian," KJ said, dropping his head in shame.

Ian could tell that Andrea's words had hurt his nephew. "Hey," Ian said, rubbing KJ's shoulder, "you don't have to own that. Don't you dare drop your head because of what someone else did. I don't care if it's your mother or your father. Be your own man. If you ask me, your mother is dead wrong," Ian said loud enough for his sister to hear him.

"Can you give me a few minutes to get my stuff together? I don't wanna stay here with her no more. All she does is put me down and call me names. I'm not gay, and every time she gets mad, which is all the time, she calls me a name. I just wanna get out of here," KJ said, not seeming to miss a beat from the times he used to share with his uncle when he was a small kid.

Ian nodded. "Yeah, man. Go ahead and get what you need. You can stay with me as long as you'd like."

Chapter 16

Zola was feeling better. Her facial bruises were still visible, but the pain had subsided a great deal. Whatever they gave her for her aching ribs worked, because even they were feeling so much better than just two days ago. Her doctor had finally authorized her release, and she couldn't be happier. Five days of drugs and medical attention had done wonders for her, but now it was time to get on with the rest of her life.

The police hadn't come back, nor had she heard anything from them. Her attorney, Ms. Capers, was a no-nonsense type of woman, and she must have meant it when she said that they wouldn't be bothering her again unless they had enough evidence to charge her with a crime. The mere fact that she had someone like Ms. Capers on the job allowed her to rest easier.

Now she was sitting in the prerelease area, waiting for Kecia to pick her up. While she waited, she couldn't help but think of how close she had gotten with Kecia since this incident happened. Kecia had become the little sister she had always wanted but never had.

Before she could get too deep into her thoughts, her name was called, and one of the nurses who treated her while she was there brought out a wheelchair.

"Hospital policy," the nurse said.

"I understand," Zola said. "As long as I'm leaving here and can get in my own bed, you can push me out on a gurney."

"I'm sure you're happy to leave," the nurse said as she wheeled her down the ramp to the parking area. "Good luck with everything."

"Thanks," Zola said.

"And I'm really sorry to hear about your mother," the nurse said. "I try to mind my business, but when your sister came in and told me your mother had passed, well, I didn't mind breaking the visitation rules for that. Mothers are special, and I'm really sorry to hear of your loss."

Zola nodded and pretended to be grieving, but she was thinking, *if you only knew my mother, you wouldn't be singing that tune.* "Thanks. I appreciate your condolences," Zola said.

"My name is Mimi," the nurse said. "I didn't want to be all in your business while you were a patient—besides, that's against hospital rules—but I lost my mother last year, and let me just say it's been tough."

"I'm sorry to hear that, Mimi," Zola said and couldn't help but envy whatever relationship the nurse had with her mother that would make her tear up at the mere mention of her death.

"Your sister is a very sharp young lady," Mimi said, pointing toward Kecia, who was running around the side of her Mini Cooper to open the passenger door.

"Yeah," Zola said with a smile. "I think I'll let her stick around."

"I have a surprise for you," Kecia said, smiling from ear to ear.

Before she could open the door, it opened on its own, and out stepped a little boy who was about four feet five inches tall and was wearing khaki pants and a maroon dress shirt beneath a navy blue blazer with a gold crescent on the breast pocket. The little boy smiled and ran toward Zola.

"Jason," Zola screamed so loudly they could hear her inside the hospital.

"Hi, Mom," he said with a wide smile.

"Oh, my God," Zola said as she jumped up out of the wheelchair and ran to her son. She leaned down and hugged him so tight that her ribs started hurting again. "How are you? I missed you so much, little boy."

"I missed you too," Jason said with his proper diction. "I haven't seen you in months. Are you okay?"

"I'm doing just fine," Zola said as she reached down and hugged him again. "How is it that you have Jason?" Zola asked, turning to Kecia.

"Ask him," she said with a frown.

Zola's smile disappeared, and she looked down at her son. "Jason?" she said.

Jason dropped his head. "I ran away," he said.

"You did what?" Zola said.

"I ran away. Carmen is mean," he said. "She always talks bad about you. She's not nice like she acts in front of you. She's a faker, and I don't want to live with her anymore."

"How did you get him?" Zola asked Kecia.

"He called your cell phone. Here ya go," Kecia said, reaching out to give the BlackBerry back to Zola. "He said he was at the bus stop, and I had to go get him. When I got there, he was just standing there alone. He's smart for his age, but he's still only six years old, so I wasn't about to tell him to go back."

"Yeah," Zola said, "I understand. Jason, you have to know better than that. That was very dangerous. Anything could've happened to you."

"But it didn't, and I'm with you again," he said with a child's innocence.

Zola sighed and looked around as if someone were playing a cruel joke on her. "Okay," she said, "but there are certain ways we have to do things, Jason. You can't just . . . Never mind. Let's go."

Jason jumped in the back seat, and Kecia helped Zola into the passenger's seat before running back around and jumping in on the driver's side.

"I'm hungry," Kecia said. "Lunch on me if y'all wanna eat."

"We have to get Mr. Man here back to school," Zola said, turning around in her seat and peering at her son.

"Nooo," Jason said. "I wanna stay with you."

"I know, and I want you to stay with me too, but we have to do this the right way, or I'll be in big trouble."

"Carmen said you're going to jail because you did something bad," Jason said, crossing his arms and sticking his lips out.

"Listen to me, Jason. I haven't done anything bad. Chad told me that you saw the news, but that was all one big mistake. I would never lie to you. You do know that, don't you?" Zola asked, staring into the little boy's eyes, which looked just like her own. Jason was the spitting image of his mother.

"Yes," Jason said, nodding his head but still pouting.

"Where to?" Kecia asked as she zipped out of the hospital's parking lot.

"School," Zola repeated. "We have to get Jason back to school before he gets in trouble."

"No," Jason whined. "I don't wanna go back there. I wanna stay with you."

Zola's heart raced. The last thing she wanted to do was send her son away. She always kept a strong facade, but living without Jason was something that weighed heavily on her mind daily, and now that he was here, she really wasn't in any rush to send him back.

"Why don't we do this," Zola said. "Why don't we go grab some lunch, and then I will take you back to school?"

"But I don't wanna go back to school, 'cause then, after it's over, Carmen will pick me up. Carmen is mean to you, and I hate her," Jason said.

"Don't worry about Carmen. I can take care of myself," Zola said.

"I know a secret," Jason said, looking directly into his mother's face. "If I tell you, can I stay with you?"

"A secret?" Zola asked. "What kind of secret?"

"Can we go to your house?" Jason asked, bargaining.

"For lunch, Jason. We will eat lunch, and then we are taking you back to school. I can get in big trouble behind this," Zola said.

"Okay," Jason said, pouting. "But I'm only going to run away again. I hate Carmen. She's mean."

"No," Zola said. "I'm going to do what I have to do to get you back home with me, but you have to promise me you'll help me. Do you promise?"

Jason looked out the window and nodded.

Seeing her son so sad gave Zola the extra motivation to get a plan in place to get him back under her roof.

Chapter 17

Ian pulled into his driveway around four thirty in the morning. The moon was bright, sending a calming glow over the ghetto. A police car cruised up his street and slowed down, then pointed its searchlight at Ian's truck. Ian opened the door but didn't get out of the truck. He shielded his eyes from the bright light. He waved a hand at the officer.

"Everything okay, Ian?" the officer asked.

"Yeah," Ian said to the officer he couldn't see given the bright light shining on him. "Yeah, sitting here talking to my nephew."

"Good enough," the officer said, then turned his light off and pulled away.

"It's quiet over here at night," KJ said.

"Only when the police are out," Ian said.

The presence of the police always sent the crackheads, prostitutes, and other people of the night home early. He put his Ford in park and turned to his nephew.

"Uncle Ian, I was just over here the other day. I didn't know you lived here," KJ said, looking around the hood as if he were on safari.

"What were you doing over here?" Ian asked.

"Just hanging out," he said.

"Just hanging out, huh? Who were you hanging out with?" Ian asked.

"Some friends from school," KJ said.

"Boy," Ian said, shaking his head, "you don't lie very well. But I'ma leave that one alone for now."

KJ didn't try to defend himself, which bothered Ian. If he tried to fix his lie, it would at least show he cared. But all KJ did was hunch his shoulders as if to say, "Take it or leave it."

"I don't have a guest room, so you can take Christian's room or camp out on the sofa."

KJ looked past Ian and out the window at a human figure coming quickly toward the truck. The person was walking across the neighbor's grass and onto Ian's lawn.

"Uncle Ian," KJ said, pointing behind him, "somebody's coming."

Ian turned around just in time to see Trudy rushing up to the window. "Ian," she said, motioning for him to get out of the car.

"Are you trying to get yourself shot, Trudy?" Ian asked after he pushed the button to let the window down.

"Nah," she said with her eyes wide from drugs. "I'm trying to get some money."

"Well, keep trying and watch out," he said, getting out of the truck.

"Who dat?" she asked, pointing at KJ.

"My nephew," he said. "KJ, this is Trudy. She's a friend from the neighborhood who really needs to find a job."

"Job? Hell to the no. I don't want one of them things. They might ask me to work," she said, laughing. "Nice to meet you, KJ."

KJ frowned at the shell of a woman standing before him but waved his hand. "Nice to meet you too," he said.

"Handsome li'l devil. You got a girlfriend?" Trudy asked.

"Yes, ma'am," KJ said. "I'm good."

"I bet you are," Trudy said, licking her tongue out at the minor. "Ian, you having a whole lot of family come by here lately. Where is Christian?"

"At my sister's house," he said.

"Sister? Boy, I didn't know you had a sister. Well, well, you learn something new every day. I guess that was your brother who came by here earlier."

"Brother? My brother was with me," Ian said, motioning for KJ to follow him as he made his way to the front porch.

"Oh, well, some guy came by," she said.

"What did he want?" Ian asked.

"I don't know. I didn't ask. He asked me if I seen you. But now that I think about it, he didn't say your name, just said something about your truck. He was a nice guy. Gave me a few dollars," Trudy said.

"What did he look like?" Ian asked.

"He was kind of sexy," Trudy said. "Look, I ain't got all night to be out here playing interviews now. I need to hold a few dollars until I get my check."

"What check, Trudy? You been getting a check since I've known you, and I haven't seen any kind of payment back of one dime that I've already given you."

"Oh. It's like that, Ian? Okay. I'ma remember that," Trudy said.

"Good. Please do," Ian said. "Well, we're going to call it a night. You be careful out here."

"You ain't gonna give me a few bucks?"

"Look," Ian said, "I don't mind helping you out from time to time, but I'm not going to be your automatic teller. You're going to have to get a job like everyone else."

"So you really ain't gonna give me a few dollars?" Trudy said, amazed that he was turning her down.

"Nope," he said. "I'm going to stop enabling you. You're one of the smartest people I know, and I'm not going to keep helping you get high. Check yourself into a rehab and get your life back."

"Aw, man," she said, sucking her raggedy teeth. "Here you go sounding like everybody else. I don't wanna hear that shit."

"You might not wanna hear that shit, but you need to," Ian said, opening his door. He paused to let KJ into the house, then turned to Trudy. "Good night."

"That man who came by here looking for you," she said and paused for effect, "he had a gun. I saw it with my own eyes. So you be careful."

Ian stared at the woman as she made her way down his driveway. A car drove by, and the driver slowed down when he saw Trudy. He drove a few houses down from Ian and stopped. Trudy ran up and got into the passenger's side. She was going to get her money the hard way. He wondered if she was telling the truth or just upset that he didn't give her the money she requested.

He closed the door and made sure the deadbolt was locked. He turned on the house alarm.

"Make yourself at home, nephew," he said, pointing to his son's door. "Why don't you take Christian's room and we'll talk in the morning?"

"Okay," KJ said.

Ian hit the automatic alarm on his Ford until he heard it chirp. Satisfied that his vehicle was safe, he walked back to his bedroom to retrieve his gun. He had a feeling Trudy was telling the truth about that visitor.

Chapter 18

Ravon walked down the street and barely glanced at the house where all the murder and mayhem had taken place. His mother was dead, and strangely enough, everything seemed normal on the block. He looked around at the surrounding houses and realized that life went on as if nothing had happened. Death was nothing new to the ghetto. Every single day you could find a little red light on someone's porch, letting passersby know that a family member had gone on to meet their Maker. He stopped walking and looked at the house he came to visit.

A light was on in a back room. He saw a television's blue screen dance off the living room wall. A dog barked and ran full speed at him but stopped right before he ran into the chain-link fence. He looked to his left at his mother's house and wondered where the police cars were. He couldn't help but think of how his mother looked when he saw her lying on the sofa. She seemed to have died in a lot of pain. Her mouth was twisted up into a menacing snarl, her hands were curled into little fists, and her eyes were still open. Then he remembered the blood. The floor was covered with it. He was amazed at how much blood could come from such a small woman.

Ravon took a deep breath, looked around to see if anyone was watching, and then walked up the cement stairs leading to Mrs. Ham's house. He knocked on the door and waited.

There was no answer, but he knew she was there. He knocked again. He could hear some movement inside.

"Who dat out dere?" the old woman from New Orleans asked in her heavy drawl.

"This is Ravon. Ravon from next door. Sara's son," he said.

"Hey, baaaabe," she said. "Whatcha want dis time of night?"

"I just have a quick question," he said. "I promise you I won't hold you long."

The door clicked, then opened. Mrs. Ham stood behind the screen door wearing a nightgown and a housecoat that hung on her skinny frame like it hung from a hanger. She had an array of colorful rollers in her gray hair.

"Whatcha need, chile?" she said through the bars on the window of the storm door.

"I'm sorry to come by here so late, but I'm trying to find out what happened next door," Ravon said.

"I don't know nothing but what I told the police," she said.

"What was that?" Ravon said, hoping she hadn't mentioned his name.

"The last person I seen coming from over there was your sister. That was when I saw you that day. You never went inside. You just left and went to find that girl. That's all I know," Mrs. Ham said. "Now I don't want any trouble. I like to mind my business, so I would appreciate it if you don't put me in this mess."

"That's all you know?"

"Yep," she said, backing away from the door. "Now I need to get back to bed."

"Okay," Ravon said. "Thank you for answering the door at this time of night, and I'm sorry for waking you."

Mrs. Ham nodded but stood staring at Ravon. He could tell there was something else the old woman wanted to tell him. Ravon didn't move.

"Listen," she said, "hey, there was this car that dropped your sister off. One of those truck things that I see on my cop shows. I got the license plate. I didn't give this to the police because, like I said, I like to mind my business. But you just wait right there. Now I don't know if this will help you, but you wait right there."

Ravon waited on the porch. Mrs. Ham closed her door, and Ravon heard the locks click back into place. He turned around and looked over at his mother's house. All that let on that a crime had taken place were a few strips of yellow police tape around the front door and carport. He thought back to the man he found in the house and couldn't help but wonder what kind of foolishness his mother was caught up in.

He scratched his head and wished he had better known the woman who gave birth to him. He remembered a letter she wrote to him when he was in prison. It was the only letter he received from her in the five years he was there, but it spoke volumes about what made her tick.

Dear Ravon,

I hope this letter finds you in good health and spirits. I know you didn't expect to hear from me, and to be honest with you, I don't know why I'm writing you. I guess when you give birth to somebody, you should act like you care, so I'm trying. But the truth is I never wanted kids. I don't like kids. I really don't like people. People are evil, and over the years, I think I can honestly say that I've gotten to know myself. I believe the world we live in is hell and heaven is waiting in the afterlife.

I grew up in California, and when I was a teenager, I joined the Black Panther Party for social and economic change. I met a man and fell in love. We moved to Atlanta to start a branch here, but something changed once we got here. He fell out of love with the struggle and in love with heroin. I still tried to be there for him, but he was cursed. On the day Zola was born, he left, and the only time I saw him after that was in my nightmares.

To be honest with you, I don't know who your daddy is. I was a zombie walking around and meeting men just to keep me company, but most of them were evil and selfish and mere products of this world we live in. I never met my own parents. They decided I wasn't worth sticking around for. I grew up in a California orphanage where I met hundreds, maybe even thousands, of black faces just like me. I was treated okay. No physical or sexual abuse for me, but when I turned 17, they cut me loose, and to me, that was its very own kind of abuse. They sent a skinny little girl out into that cruel world to fend for myself, and I was promptly sexually and physically abused.

That's when I joined the movement. I needed a family to protect me, and the Panthers offered that. But even that wasn't all it cracked up to be. We started out strong, but drugs were flooded into our neighborhoods, and we weren't smart enough to avoid it. Over the years, seeing how my people have virtually destroyed their lives, I took on the notion to help them finish the job.

Everywhere I turn, I see black faces who don't care anything about prosperity or their families. There is no self-love. The folks who have money look down on the ones who don't, and the ones who don't have it hate the ones who have it, so they rob and kill and rape and so on and so on. I bet if you take a look around that prison you are in, you will see mostly black faces. Why do you think that's the case? Black people are cursed.

You've always been a good boy, yet you are sitting there with some of the world's worst. Why do you think that's the case? You've always gotten good grades, you even got a few academic scholarship offers, but where are you? And why? If you were any other race, the judge would've slapped you on the wrist and said, "Don't do that anymore," but you are black, and probation just wouldn't do. I can't tell you the number of times I wanted to just kill us all because this world isn't meant for us. Don't you worry. I'm not going to commit suicide or anything. I believe in my own Higher Power, and that is one of the sins that I think is unforgivable.

Well, I just wanted to write you and let you know who I really am. I'm not a bad person. I'm just a cursed one.

Sara

P.S. If you talk to your sister, tell her I don't hate her, but I'm not fit to be anyone's mother. Medication altered my way of thinking when I did what I did to her, and I will never forgive myself for that, but she has to move on and live her life. She came by here a few days ago, but I just couldn't bring myself to open the door. She's a big-hearted girl, and I really hate myself even more when I see her. I'm full of evil spirits, son. And that was an evil spirit that tried to ruin her from having any kids. Crazy as it sounds, I was trying to look out for her. So pray for me. Pray for us all. God has a special place for us.

"Baaabe," Mrs. Ham said, bringing Ravon back to the here and now, "here is the paper I wrote the license plate number on. I didn't give this to the police because something told me not to. You can't trust them, and the ones they sent around here seemed a little crooked."

"Hard to find a good one," Ravon said.

"Yeah. I always listen to my first thought, but maybe you can do something with it and find out if that man knows something. I didn't get along with Sara too well, but she didn't deserve that."

Ravon thought about how the two women would stare at each other and never utter a word, one not liking the other for no apparent reason except for the need for drama.

"Thanks, Mrs. Ham," Ravon said, staring down at the paper and trying to make out the chicken scratches she called writing. "Is this a G or an O?"

Mrs. Ham laughed, squinted her wrinkled eyelids, then shook her head. "I don't know."

"Okay," he said. "I'll figure it out. You take care of yourself now."

"I sho' will," she said. "I'm glad you taking care of your momma. She was a mean old bitch, but she was still yo' momma."

"Yeah." Ravon nodded and turned to walk down the steps of the front porch. "You be careful around here."

"I will," she said. "And you do the same. Hey, Ravon."

"Yes, ma'am," he said, stopping and turning around to face her.

"I saw you leaving the house the other day. It was right after I heard those gunshots," she said, pointing her bony finger at him.

Ravon stared at the woman without saying a word. His heart hit the floor. The first thing he thought about was going back to prison. That wasn't going to happen. Her next words would decide if she lived or died. He had killed once and really didn't feel the slightest bit of remorse, and he was sure this kill wouldn't cause him much discomfort either.

"But they say yo' momma was stabbed to death. And the white man was shot. If there is one thing I know about yo' momma, she didn't have too much love in her heart for white peoples. So I know that cracker wasn't making no social call. So I had to ask myself, what was his pale ass doing up in there? I say that to say your secret is safe with me. I don't blame you for what you done, and you ain't got to worry about me telling a soul."

Ravon grunted and nodded his head. He wasn't sure if she was wearing a wire and working for the police. He wasn't saying anything to incriminate himself. "You take care of yourself, Mrs. Ham."

"Oh, don't you worry about me. You take care of yourself. And I hope your momma is finally at peace," she said, closing her door and sliding all the locks into place.

Chapter 19

Zola opened the door to her condominium and stepped back to allow Jason and Kecia to enter before her.

"I need to grab a few things, and then I can get my butt to work," Kecia said as she made a beeline to the guest room.

"I thought you were off today," Zola said as she looked around her place.

"I am, but I'm a student, girl. Do you know how much work I have to do? I'm never really off. When I'm off, I'm studying, and when I'm working, I'm studying. Besides, I never liked being a third wheel. You guys need to spend some time together. I have plenty to keep me busy," she said as she disappeared.

Jason walked around and checked out his mom's place. He walked over by the large wall-length window and looked down at the cars below racing up and down Moreland Avenue. "I wanna stay here," he said to no one in particular. "I don't want to go back over there with them."

Zola heard the pain in her son's voice and felt helpless to do anything to ease it. She knew she couldn't just pick up the phone and call the Benjamins and tell them, "I'll take it from here."

Kecia rushed out of the guest room, then turned around and went right back. She came out and said her goodbyes to both of them. Zola waved her hand, but her attention was on Jason. Their eyes met, and Zola saw his eyes begging her to save him. But what happened? The last few times she visited him, he seemed to be enjoying himself so much that she walked away feeling like she was in the way of his life.

Zola walked over to the window and stood beside Jason. "I really want you to stay with me too, Jason," she said. "But things are a little complicated. Will you tell me why you don't want to stay with the Benjamins anymore?"

"They are not nice. Well, Chad is, but Carmen is mean. She always talks about you. She told me that I wasn't going to see you ever again and that I needed to get used to it. She drinks a lot. She's weird. I don't like her."

"Has she ever hit you?" Zola asked.

"No," Jason said, shaking his head. "She just keeps saying she loves me, and she doesn't want you to have me."

"Well, you have been with them for a long time, and she probably does love you," Zola said.

"I know, but I'm your son. I'm not their son. Do you have a room for me?"

There was something about the way he said that that made her want to cry.

"Of course," she said. "You are my son. It doesn't matter where you're spending your days and nights. I'll always have a room for you. Why do you think I got a two-bedroom place? One for me and one for you," she said with a smile.

Jason smiled too and hugged his mother's waistline. Something caught his eye, and he pulled away and walked over to the coffee table. He picked up a picture frame and stared at it. Inside the frame was a picture of Zola and Andre.

"Why do you have a picture of Mr. Marvin?" he asked.

Zola frowned. *Mr. Marvin?* "Who?" she asked. "His name is Andre, and he's my friend."

"No," Jason said, shaking his head. "That's Mr. Marvin, and he works for the Benjamins. He used to be the driver. He used to take me to school every day, but now he does something else."

"Jason, are you sure that this is the same guy?" Zola said, taking the picture from him and pointing at Andre.

"Yes," Jason said. "He has a cut over his lip. He told me he got that playing football."

He told me he got it in a car accident, she thought.

"He was at the house before I left. Somebody beat him up, and I overheard him arguing with Carmen. He was telling her he wasn't going to do something, and she got mad. I mean really mad. Then he left."

Zola's heart hit the carpet as she wondered what Andre could possibly have to do with Carmen.

Zola walked over and turned on the television. "What's your favorite show?" she asked while handing him the remote control.

"*Everybody Hates Chris,* but it's not on," Jason said, taking a seat on the plush leather sofa.

"Well, have at it. I need to make a phone call," she said as she went into her bedroom.

Zola grabbed her cell phone and called Sharon Capers, the attorney, and explained her situation. She told her about what Jason said about "Andre" and the coincidence of him beating her then ending up at the Benjamins, arguing with Carmen. Sharon told her that she would look into it, but in the meantime, she should get Jason back over to the Benjamins.

"I can't do that," Zola said. "I think he may be in danger."

"Well, then we need to get the police involved. And you said you never relinquished full custody?" Sharon responded. "Only temporary, right?"

"Right," Zola said. "I would never give up the rights to my child. That would never happen in a million years. I don't care how poor I was or how rich the Benjamins are. That's my son."

"Okay. I understand," Sharon said. "In the meantime, you call the police and tell them you believe Jason is in danger. You tell them everything that you know. Don't hold back anything to try to protect this 'Andre' guy because it's pretty obvious that he's not who he said he is and he's working for her. You're still his mother, and you have rights. I will have a private investigator look into the Benjamins, and if you hear or can think of anything that might help build a case against them, let me know. It doesn't matter how small or insignificant you may think it is. Let me know."

"Okay," Zola said.

"Hang in there, Zola. I know you've been through a lot, but you're a fighter, and if there is anything worth fighting for, it's your son," Sharon said.

"You're right about that," she said. "And thanks again, Sharon. You're the best."

"Don't mention it," Sharon said.

Zola ended the call with the attorney and sat on the edge of her bed. Everything she had with Andre was a lie. He was a liar. She felt like a fool for some of the things she did for him all in the name of love. All kinds of emotions raced through her body: fear, anger, resentment, embarrassment, hate, but the one that kept overriding the others was pain. She had been used once again. Tears formed in the corners of her eyes and raced down her cheeks.

Her mind drifted back to the crazy lady who was screaming at her the day she left Sara's house.

Was she really cursed?

All of a sudden Zola was happy that she insisted that the deed to the condo and the title to the car both be placed in her name when "Andre" bought them. She now had a car and a condo that were paid for, and all because the Benjamins wanted her out of the picture. She was going to make sure she stayed one step ahead of them. She looked at her BlackBerry, then sighed. It was time. She dialed 911. It was time to get this situation resolved once and for all.

"Nine one one, what's your emergency?"

"My son is in danger," Zola said in a calm and cool fashion. There was a peace that ran through her veins like never before. "There are some very wealthy and powerful people who want to take him from me. I need to speak with a police officer right now."

Chapter 20

Ravon sat with his eyes trained on the house across the street. It was almost four in the morning, and he had been sitting there for two hours. After he left Mrs. Ham's house, he got a stroke of luck when Lisa called. He had her pull the license plate number that the old woman had just gotten. He wasn't sure how she did it, but she called him back with an address and the owner's name. It didn't take long for him to find the place because the West End area of Atlanta was where he spent lots of time as a kid. He backed into the driveway of an abandoned house across the street from the one that might help him solve the riddle of who killed Sara.

His mind was racing a million miles a minute when, all of a sudden, the man's Ford Explorer pulled into the driveway. Ravon's hands began to sweat as he sat there watching. There was someone in the passenger's side, but they didn't get out of the car.

There was that woman again, the same woman who had begged him for money when he knocked on the door. He gave her $5 and asked her a few softball questions about what kind of guy was the man who owned the house. She claimed she didn't know him, but there she was again. He was willing to bet that she was warning him.

He gripped his pistol and prepared himself for the unknown. This man may have the answers to the questions that were running rampant through his mind, or was he just a Good Samaritan as Zola claimed he was?

The man got out of the vehicle with another male, and they walked into the house as the woman skittered away. The man paused before going into his house and looked up and down the street. Ravon slumped down in the driver's seat to avoid the man's gaze. He wasn't sure if the man saw him. He wasn't sure what he was going to do now that he had found the man who had dropped his sister off at Sara's house, but he needed to talk to him. He leaned his seat back and waited. As much as he wanted to get out and knock on the man's door, he knew he was taking a chance of getting shot if he slipped up.

Chapter 21

Ian turned the television off and picked up a book called *Say You Are One of Them,* a book of short stories about his people in Africa and some of the things they were going through on a daily basis. The story he was reading was called "Fattening the Gabon," a very interesting story of an uncle who had a change of heart about selling his niece and nephew to a group of child traffickers. He always enjoyed reading, novels and collections of stories in particular. The written word had always had a way of helping him to forget about the many problems that were always present between his ears. So every night before he went to sleep, he made sure to read a few chapters of some of this world's best griots.

He read until his eyes got heavy, and once he couldn't read another sentence, he reached over and placed his book on the nightstand and turned off the light. As he lay there, he couldn't help but think about the night he had with his family. In one night, he experienced all the things he really missed about his family: laughter, good food, great conversation, drama, and just plain family love. He smiled when he thought about how happy Christian was running around his sister's house. He reached over and picked up his cell phone and dialed her number.

"Hello," Andrea said in a sleepy voice.

"Did I wake you?"

"Yeah," she said. "Is everything okay? Is KJ all right?"

He was happy to hear the concern in her voice about her son. "Yeah," he said, "he's fine. Did Christian wake up?"

"No," she said. "But I'll tell you what. If he kicks me one more time, I'm going to pick up his li'l butt and put him in KJ's stink room."

Ian laughed. "Yeah, he sleeps wild."

"What you doing calling here this time of morning?"

"I was just checking on you guys."

"Stop lying, boy. You were checking to see if Christian woke up wanting you. He's not thinking about you."

"Yes, he is. He's dreaming about me right now," Ian said.

"I'm sure he is. Now if you don't mind, I'd like to get back to dreaming about Denzel Washington."

"Okay," Ian said with a grunt. "Tomorrow—well, later today—we need to talk about the way you've been treating KJ."

"The way I've been treating KJ?" Andrea almost yelled. "Ian, you've been missing in action for a long time. Don't let that boy fool you. He's not as innocent as he makes himself out to be."

"I don't care about any of that. What I do care about is the way his mother is carrying on."

"You got a lot of nerve popping your tail up and pointing fingers at me. I've been through hell and high water trying to make sure that boy has a good life, and all he does is give me his butt to kiss."

"Andrea," Ian said, "I'm not about to get into any of that. You are projecting, and I don't like it. Every time you see KJ, you see his dad. And you can't seem to get over what his dad did. I know you're angry, but you have to stop beating up on him because of the sins of his father."

"Oh, you are so wrong. I beat up on KJ because KJ acts like an ass ninety percent of the time."

"Have you ever wondered why? Have you ever tried to see things from his perspective? He got shafted in this deal too. It's not all about you. As a matter of fact, this doesn't have a damn thing to do with you. His dad didn't just leave you for another man. He left him, too. And for a son, that has to be hard."

Andrea sighed on the other end of the phone as if she wasn't trying to hear Ian's logic.

"Cut the boy some slack," Ian said. "It's bad enough he has to live with the fact that his father left him, but he left to be with another man. And on top of that, his mother is treating him like shit. Now if you need some time to yourself, he can stay with me."

There was silence on the other end, so he went on.

"You don't have to make a decision right now, but just know that I'm here. And I'm also not going to allow you to mistreat him anymore."

"I hear ya, Ian. I'm sleepy. Good night," Andrea said before hanging up.

Ian held the phone in his hand and wished he hadn't been such a stranger. His nephew was over there getting mentally abused by his scorned mother, and he knew nothing about it. He placed his phone on the nightstand and stared up at the ceiling, which was illuminated by the fading moon.

Ian's mind shifted to the guy who was asking questions about him. He wondered if he was still parked across the street. Who was he? Why was he asking Trudy about him? Was Trudy lying just to get a few bucks out of him? No, that wasn't like her. Was he a trick getting his rocks off with one of the many crackheads who strolled up and down Ralph David Abernathy Boulevard, or was he a threat? He slid his hand under his mattress and removed his 9 mm pistol.

When Ian looked at the clock again, it was almost six. He was tired, but this guy had his mind racing, so he stood up and walked to the front of his house to see if the watcher was still there. He peered through the wooden shades over the bay window and saw that the guy's car was still there. He wasn't being very inconspicuous. Ian decided he would sit back and let this guy come to him. He walked back to his room and got back into bed. It didn't take long for him to drift off into a sound and peaceful sleep.

Chapter 22

Ravon opened his eyes and was surprised to see that the night had already given way to the morning. His windows were foggy, and he was freezing. He got out of his car to stretch his legs and get a breath of fresh air. He turned and stared at the house across the street. The SUV was still in the driveway, and all the lights inside were off. His bladder was begging to be relieved, so he walked toward the back of the empty house where he'd parked, and he unzipped his pants.

"Good morning," a voice said, startling him.

Ravon whipped his head around and stared at a man who was standing on the steps of the deck. He fiddled around for his gun but realized he'd left it in the car.

"My name is Willie. What the hell is yours?"

Ravon's eyes left the man's haggard-looking face and found the long silver samurai sword he was holding as if he was going to swing it at his neck if he didn't get the answer to his question. Ravon zipped back up and ran back to his car. When he opened the door, he searched for the gun he had left on the passenger seat, but it was gone.

"You looking for this?" Harry said, holding Ravon's pistol.

"Man," Ravon said, outnumbered and outgunned. "What y'all want?"

"I wanna know why you've been hanging in my driveway all night long."

"I was sleeping, and I didn't know this was your house. I thought it was empty," Ravon said.

"That's what you get for thinking," Willie said.

"I wanna know why you asking questions about my friend," Harry said.

"Who?" Ravon asked with a frown.

"Who?" Willie snapped, pointing the sword at Ravon. "Who in the hell have you been asking about?"

"I . . . I . . ." Ravon stammered. Even though the old men seemed like harmless bums, he was petrified of the one man making a mistake with the sword.

"'I . . . I . . .' Hell. Get ya lies straight, fool," Willie said.

"Ain't nobody gonna hurt you," Harry said, waving Ravon's gun in his face.

"Speak for yourself. I ain't take my damn meds, and I'm a li'l fucked up in the head right now, so I wouldn't put it past me to take this damn sword and chop ya li'l narrow ass up and get away with it because all these police around here know I'm a li'l off," Willie said as he lifted the sword up over his head. "Now, I'ma ask you one more time. Whatcha want?"

"Whoa, man. I'm not looking for any trouble. Somebody killed my mother, and I just want to know who that guy was because he dropped my sister off at her house. My sister and my mother don't speak, so it's just odd, and all I wanted to do was ask him some questions to see if he could help lead me in the right direction," Ravon said.

"Well, we don't have no killers on this block," Willie snapped.

"Yeah, we do," Harry corrected him. "Mrs. Hazel's son, Bobby, killed those folks that time he tried to rob the check-cashing joint over there on Martin Luther King."

"And his ass is underneath the jail," Willie said. "And why you snitching, man?"

"He ain't locked up no more," Harry said. "I saw him last week at the laundromat."

"What the hell you doing at the laundromat?" Willie asked as if Ravon weren't there anymore.

"What the hell you think I'm doing at the laundromat? What people do at the laundromat, Willie?"

"I know what people do, but what the hell you doing there? You wear the same dirty-ass shirt every day."

"Ya momma wear the same drawers," Harry snapped.

"Hey," Willie said, turning his sword on Harry, "my momma is dead."

"Well, hell. I know for sure she wearing the same drawers," Harry said.

"Hey," Ravon said, raising his hand like he was in grade school.

"What?" Willie said, turning back to Ravon.

"Can I leave?"

"Hell no. We ain't done with you. Now if you wanted to talk to the man, why didn't you just walk yo' li'l ass over there and knock on the door?"

"Yeah," Harry added. "Why you out here looking all like you tryin'a rob somebody? We don't play that. We keep this street safe."

"I'm not trying to rob anybody," Ravon said.

"Of course you gonna say that. I ain't ever met a nukka who admitted to tryin'a rob somebody. You think we some kind of fools?"

"No," Ravon said, "it's not like that. I'm telling y'all the truth."

Willie looked at Harry while still holding the sword above his head. "You believe this fool?"

Harry leaned in close to Ravon's face, and Ravon backed up due to the stench coming from the bum's raggedy mouth.

"Yeah," Harry said, "I think he's telling the truth. I'm keeping this gun, but I think he's telling the truth. We don't need to kill him."

Willie lowered his weapon and smiled at Ravon. "I'll tell you what," Willie said. "You do realize we got the drop on ya, don't you?"

"I guess so," Ravon said.

"You got some money?" Willie asked.

"I have a few bucks," Ravon said.

"How much is a few bucks?" Harry added.

"About fifty dollars," Ravon said, figuring that number would satisfy them.

"Okay," Willie said. "Get in the car. We going to IHOP, and you buying, damn it. I got a taste for some of those sweet-ass pancakes."

"Huh?" Ravon said.

"You heard me, damn it," Willie said, lifting his sword again. "We kidnapping yo' ass and making you take us to breakfast."

"Yeah," Harry said. "I want some French toast and bacon. And maybe we can answer some of your questions."

"I ain't answering shit," Willie said. "I already let this fool live."

"Don't pay him no mind," Harry said. "He wasn't lying about not taking them meds."

"Man," Ravon said with a frown, "why don't I just give y'all the money and y'all go on your own?"

"Nope," Willie said. "You taking us."

"I don't have time," Ravon said.

"You got time to die?" Willie snapped.

Ravon shook his head and wondered what in the world he had gotten himself into.

Chapter 23

The morning sun was creeping through Zola's window as she rolled over and looked at her sleeping son. During the night he slept peacefully while easing closer to her. So much was on her mind that she didn't sleep very well. She felt as if she were stealing her own child because every little bump in the night sent her into a panic. She had called the police to report her concerns about Jason's welfare just as her attorney had instructed her to do, but that didn't make her feel any better. Now another day was upon them, and she could only imagine what it would bring.

Zola reached over to the nightstand and unplugged her cell phone from the charger. She looked at the screen of her BlackBerry and noticed that she had eleven missed calls, and all of them were from Carmen Benjamin. She checked her voicemail and heard Carmen's panic-filled voice.

"Zola, Jason has disappeared. We have an Amber Alert out. We are doing everything we can to locate him. He walked away from school today, and no one has seen him. Oh, my God. I'm so scared," she said. Then her voice changed as if she had a change of heart. "I hope he's not with you. If you took my son—that's right, I said 'my son'—you will regret the day you were ever born." Six or seven more messages followed with similar words.

Zola looked back at her son and leaned down and kissed his forehead. She stood and walked down the hallway. She stuck her head into the guest room to see if Kecia was up, but the room was empty, and the bed was already made.

She walked into the kitchen and poured herself a glass of orange juice. Just as she was about to swallow, her cell phone rang.

"Hello," she said.

"Zola. Are you okay?"

"Ravon?" she asked. "Where have you been?"

"Man," he said with an exasperated breath, "don't even ask. How are you?"

"I'm fine. I called you a million times. I needed a ride to the hospital."

"Damn," he said. "I'm sorry, Zo. I was with Lisa, and I promised her when I was locked up that I would spend a few days with her with no distractions. Then I lost my cell phone. Are you okay?"

"I'm getting there. Did you hear about Sara?"

"Yeah," he said. "What's going on? I need to talk to you in person. I don't trust these phones."

"I understand. Those sorry police officers showed up to the hospital room and tried to pin it on me. I didn't have anything to do with that crap. I have an attorney though, so hopefully she can straighten this out. Sara gives me hell even in death."

"Can you meet me somewhere?"

"I have Jason here, and I'm still not really comfortable driving. Why? What's going on?"

"I don't know," he said, sounding a bit panicky. "Maybe I shouldn't be out and about. Next they will be trying to pin it on me. I'm not going back to prison. Fuck that."

"Are you okay, Ray? You sound strange."

"Yeah, I'm straight. Listen, I will be in touch with you. I gotta figure some things out."

There was a knock on the door.

"Ray," Zola said as she stood and made her way over to the door, "someone's at my door."

"I'll check on you a little later. Give Jason a hug for me."

"Okay," she said as she ended the call.

Zola looked through the tiny peephole and frowned at what was on the other side of her door. She opened the door and looked into the eyes of Detective Shilo. She looked to his left and right for his pessimistic partner, but the detective was alone.

"May I come in?" he asked.

"I didn't kill anybody," she snapped. "And I would appreciate it if y'all left me alone."

"I know," he said, holding up his hands to fend off the verbal onslaught that was coming his way.

"If you know that, then why are you here harassing me?"

"I'm not. I only want to ask you a few questions," he said. "I'm here of my own accord. I'm not here to harass you or accuse you of anything. I don't approve of my partner's methods one bit, but he's been on the force way longer than I have, so I have to play my position. But I would like to have a few words with you if you don't mind."

Zola stared into the man's eyes, and he seemed sincere. She backed away from the door and allowed him to enter. She kept her mean face on and made sure he knew that he was on a short clock.

"Make it quick. I have things to do," she said. She walked to her bedroom to check on her son. He was awake now and sitting on the floor, watching television. She gave him a wave, then closed the door.

"I'll try not to take up too much of your time, Ms. Zaire," Detective Shilo said when she returned. He walked over to the end table and picked up the picture of Andre. "How well do you know this man?"

"I guess not as well as I thought I did," she said. "Why?"

"Is this the same man?" Detective Shilo said as he produced his own picture.

Zola studied the picture of the man who claimed he loved her. Both of his eyes were swollen, his top lip was almost doubled in size, and there was a nasty cut across his nose.

"Yeah," she said, nodding. "That looks like him."

"Thank you," Shilo said as he slid the picture back into his suit's breast pocket. He looked at her as if she might share a little more information.

"Is that it?"

"He paid us a visit this morning. Someone or something got a hold of him, and he was scared out of his mind."

That got her attention.

"He shared some things, but I know he's holding back."

"Did he kill my mother?"

"I don't think so," Detective Shilo said, shaking his head. "But then again, I don't know. He kept mumbling something about how he didn't sign up for people getting killed. He said 'people.' Last I checked your mother was only one person. We only found one body at the crime scene, but there was another person who died in that house. We have gunshot casings and lots of blood in the kitchen. Too much blood for the person to have survived, so somebody moved the other body."

Zola stared at the man, hanging on to his every word. She couldn't bring herself to mourn her mother, but she was still interested in how she met her demise.

"Your friend here," Detective Shilo said, tapping the frame, "I think he knows more than he's telling, and some of the things he's saying are lies. Which is why I'm here. How long have you known Mr. Dubois?"

"Not long enough to know that was his last name. What is his first?"

"Andy. Andy Dubois. He's from Cleveland, Ohio. He did a few years in prison for various petty crimes. He likes to find wealthy women and prey on them."

"Well, I'm far from wealthy."

"I know," he said and swept his eyes around the opulent pad and nodded his head. "You were not his target, but from the looks of this place you have here, you seem to be doing okay for yourself."

"Who was his target?"

"That's why I'm here. I need a little help. The people who keep your son, what kind of relationship do you have with them?"

I thought I had a pretty good one until that bitch tried to poison my son against me, she thought, but since he was a police officer, and she didn't trust anyone who worked for the judicial system, she just hunched her shoulders. "My son told me he works for the people who are caring for him. He said he heard him arguing with Carmen."

"And Carmen is his foster mother?" Detective Shilo said as he pulled out his mini writing pad.

"She's just a caregiver. I'm my son's mother."

"I see," Detective Shilo said, nodding his head. "Well, Mr. Dubois claims he wanted to stop working for her. But when I asked him what he did for her, he started stuttering."

"Why did he come to you?"

"He seems to think someone is trying to kill him. He said his car blew up and he was kidnapped, beaten, and left for dead. I haven't been able to confirm the car story, but his broken arm and leg and facial lacerations say he might be telling the truth."

"I see," Zola said, shaking her head at what she was hearing. "What does all of this have to do with me? Do you think I tried to kill him, too?"

"Nope," Detective Shilo said. "I thought I was clear when I said I wasn't here to accuse you of anything."

"So all you wanted to know was how I knew Andre? Or Andy, whatever you said his name was?"

"And anything else you could tell me."

"I can tell you that I don't think my child is safe with Carmen Benjamin, and I'm not sending him back over there."

Detective Shilo nodded as if to say he worked homicide, not domestic cases. "Thank you for your time, Ms. Zaire, and I hope you get better soon."

Zola nodded and walked him to the door. Just as she opened the door, two hulking uniformed police officers stood staring at her with stern faces. The white officer wore shades and had a crew cut. The black guy was dark as the night and seemed to be ready to shoot her.

"Zola Zaire, we're here to pick up Jason Zaire," the black officer said. "You are in violation of a court order, and if you don't produce the child, you will be arrested for kidnapping."

Zola looked at Detective Shilo for help, but he was already walking down the hallway toward the elevator.

"You're not taking my son," Zola said.

"Ma'am, please step aside," crew cut said.

"I can't do that," she said. "I just called the police and explained to them that my child is in danger."

"Ma'am, we're not going to ask you again," the black guy said as he removed his Taser.

Zola looked into the man's eyes and couldn't find a trace of compassion. She pushed the door closed, and crew cut caught it with his black steel-toe boot. The black officer stuck his hand through the door and let off 50,000 volts of electricity directly into her already-frail body.

The shock was like something she had never felt before. Her entire body locked up and felt as if was about to go into cardiac arrest. She lay on the floor helplessly as the two officers rushed in and went to her bedroom. When she looked up, crew cut was carrying her son in his arms. Jason looked around, then noticed his mother on the floor and started screaming.

"Mom," the little boy screamed. "Mommmmmmmm."

The sound was heart-wrenching, but she couldn't move to do anything to stop them. The black officer stood over her, staring down like he had just stepped on a roach. Zola looked up at him and pleaded with her eyes for him to leave her child with her, but all he did was give her a blank stare in return. She tried to speak, but her brain didn't seem to get the message. The next thing she heard was the door closing, and her son was gone.

Chapter 24

Ian worked his way around the kitchen. He was cooking a late brunch of grits, eggs, turkey sausage, and raisin toast. After he poured two glasses of orange juice, he walked into Christian's room and knocked on the already-open door.

"Good morning, KJ."

KJ rolled over and looked around as if he were in a bad dream. He jerked his head from left to right, and then he settled on his uncle. He squinted as he zeroed in on the familiar-looking face.

"Hey," he said, finally finding his bearings.

"It's time to rise and shine, my man. Washcloths are in the bathroom on the shelf. I've already cooked, so hop to it before your food gets cold."

KJ rolled over and sat on the side of the bed. He looked around the room and saw a slew of toy cars on a desk. He smiled and remembered when he was a toy fanatic. His dad would buy him anything he would ever dream of. He stood and sighed at how drastically things had changed between him and the man who meant everything to him.

KJ walked to the bathroom and relieved himself, then washed his hands and face. He used the brand-new toothbrush that was sitting on the marble countertop before walking out into the kitchen.

"Good afternoon," Ian said. "I hope you're hungry."

"Yeah," KJ said. "I'm starving."

"Good," Ian said as he placed a loaded plate in front of his nephew and took a seat across from him.

"How long can I stay with you?" KJ asked.

"How long would you like to stay?"

"Forever," he said. "My mother hates me, and my dad doesn't even care enough to hate me."

"That's not true. Both your parents love you."

"You can love someone and not like them. Like, I love my mom, but I don't like her. I don't like my dad, and I'm not sure I even love him."

"You and your dad were always very close, so I think you are just angry or disappointed with him. Like you said, you can love and not like."

"Yeah," KJ said as he dropped his head and said grace.

"Is that why you are dabbling in drugs?"

KJ's eyes got as wide as silver dollars.

"Yeah," Ian said. "You didn't think you were hiding it, did you?"

KJ didn't answer.

"Well, I'm not going to sit here and preach but make that your last time doing that. Just because you're not happy with the way things are going in your life doesn't mean you quit living. And when you dabble in drugs, you check out of life."

There was a loud commotion out on the front porch. Ian wiped his mouth with a cloth napkin and stood up. He walked out through the living room and opened the door.

"What's going on out here, fellas?"

Willie and Harry were flanking some guy who looked like he wanted to strangle both of them.

"What's going on? I'll tell ya what's going on. This man here says you murdered his mother," Harry said.

"No, he didn't," Willie said. "He said he wanted to talk to Ian because Ian knows who murdered his mother. Damn, Harry, get ya facts straight."

"I didn't say either one of those things. And get y'all hands off me. I already took y'all to IHOP and the liquor store. Now will y'all let me talk to this man in peace?"

Willie looked at Harry as if to see if it was okay to release their prisoner.

"Give me five dollars and I'll let you go," Harry said.

"I ain't giving y'all another dime, and get your dirty hands off me."

"Hey, hey, hey," Ian said. "I'll take it from here, guys."

Willie held up his hands, and Harry held out his. "Five dollars, nukka?"

"Bye, Harry," Ian said. "I'll make sure I give you a li'l something a little later."

The two drunks left the porch, and Ian walked out to join the visitor. He looked out into the street and noticed the same car parked out by his mailbox as the one he saw earlier.

"What's up?"

"My name is Ravon Zaire, and I understand you dropped my sister off at my mom's house. My mom ended up killed, and I was wondering if you knew anything that might help me find out what's going on. I'll be honest with you, I just got out of prison, and I don't trust the police. She said you were nice to her."

Ian stared at the guy, not sure what to think. "How did you know who I was?"

"The lady next door gave me your license plate number," Ravon said.

"How is your sister doing?"

"She's okay. What can you tell me? I'm afraid the police are going to try to pin this on me."

"Why would they do that?"

"Because I'm an easy target."

"I see," Ian said. "Well, the only thing I did was drop her off. Some clown was chasing her, and she ran into the street. I almost hit her."

"She said she gave you a key."

"She did," Ian said, nodding. "I took the key, went into her place. The man was still assaulting her, and I put a stop to that. She was in pretty bad shape, but she gave me her mother's address, and I took her there, and that's the last time I saw her. Well, with the exception of seeing her picture on the news. Seems they arrested her or are looking at her about that situation with your mom."

Ravon sighed. "Is that all you know?"

"That's it," Ian said and looked up to see a motorcycle racing down his street. There were two people, both wearing black, on the sports bike, and one was riding backward. That was strange. "Oh, shit."

Pow. Pow. Pow. Pow. Pow. Pow. Pow.

Ian jumped back behind his door and hit the floor. Once the shooting had ceased, he stuck his arm out the door and grabbed Ravon's leg, pulling him into the house.

Ian looked back to make sure KJ was okay and noticed the boy still sitting at the table with his fork stopped midway to his mouth. "Get down, boy," Ian snapped. He turned his attention back to Ravon. "Are you hit?"

"No," Ravon said.

Ian jumped up and ran to his bedroom to retrieve his own gun. He chambered a round and walked back out to the living room.

"Call nine one one," he said to KJ, then turned to Ravon. "And you come with me."

They walked out onto the porch, and Ian looked down the street where the motorcycle had gone but didn't see anything.

"What kind of foolishness are you bringing to me, boy?"

"Nobody knows I'm over here. Maybe they're after you," Ravon said.

Ian ignored him and continued to walk down his street toward where the bike had gone. As he walked,

he thought he noticed something in the middle of the
street. He strained his eyes and realized that it was
the bike lying on its side. Both men picked up their pace
until they reached the carnage. Willie and Harry were
standing by the two men. The bike was a little farther
down, and beside it was a bloody sword. One of the men,
who wore black leather, was lying in the street with a
deep laceration across his chest. Blood was pouring from
his cut, and he was lying on his back, grimacing in pain.
The other rider was sitting up with his hands behind his
head as if he were about to be arrested by Harry, who had
a gun trained on him. One of the men was white and the
other one was black.

"Good Lord," Ian said as he watched the man's blood
rush from his body.

"Didn't I tell you we take care of this block?" Willie said
to Ravon. "These yo' friends?"

"No," Ravon said as he studied the face of the white
man. "I don't know who they are."

"Who the hell y'all shooting at?" Willie asked the white
guy with the long ponytail. He didn't respond.

Ian walked over to ponytail and kneeled down. "What's
the problem?" he whispered.

"Just doing my job," ponytail said.

"What job is that?"

"Is your name Ian?"

"Yep."

"To kill you."

"Who wants me dead?"

"It's not important," the man said. "I'll never tell."

"Oh, yes, the hell you will," Willie said as he walked
over and picked up his sword. "Or I will chop your
muthafucking head off."

Ponytail looked up with pure, unadulterated fear in his
eyes.

Willie lifted the sword over his head. "You got to the count of three, damn it. One, two—"

"Do it," the man said with a straight face.

Two police cars came rushing down the street toward them, forcing Willie to put down his weapon. He nodded toward Harry, and they casually walked away from the crime scene as if they didn't have a care in the world.

Chapter 25

Zola was on her feet and rushing to her bedroom to get dressed. She cursed words she didn't know were in her as she threw on a pair of workout tights, a hooded sweatshirt, and a pair of Nike running shoes. Her cell phone rang, and she looked at the caller ID. It was Kecia.

"They took Jason," she yelled into the phone. "Can you call the attorney for me? I'm going to get my son."

"I thought I just saw the police leave here with him. Oh, my God. I will call her now. Where are you going?"

"Out to the Benjamins'. They are not keeping my son. I never gave them custody. I don't know what kind of lie that bitch told those assholes who came in here," Zola said as she grabbed her car keys from the hook on the kitchen wall.

"I'll call Sharon right now, but please don't do anything that will get you in trouble."

Zola ended the call without a response. She ran back to her bedroom and lifted her mattress. She grabbed her silver .32 automatic handgun and tossed it into her purse. There was no limit to how far she was willing to go in order to bring her child home.

Zola raced from her condo and decided the elevator was too slow. She ran down the hallway and hit the emergency exit, taking the stairs two at a time. Kecia was waiting for her when she reached the lobby.

"I called Sharon, and she told me to tell you not to go out there," Kecia said to Zola but was totally ignored.

Zola rushed out into the parking lot, bumping into an old white couple and knocking their groceries to the ground. She didn't bother to apologize as she ran and jumped into the Jaguar. Once the ignition was started, she raced out of the parking garage and onto Moreland Avenue without looking. A car slammed on its brakes and just barely missed her. The driver screamed profanities at her, but Zola was gone.

The weekends were always great for driving, and highway I-20 was clear. Zola pressed the gas on the high-powered sports car and was doing over one hundred miles per hour in a matter of seconds. She had tunnel vision and was totally focused on getting her son back. She made it to Georgia State Route 400 in no time and took the north ramp out to Alpharetta where the Benjamins lived.

She looked into her rearview mirror and saw a police car coming up. She eased off the gas pedal and looked down at her speedometer. She was doing seventy miles per hour. Zola moved over into the far-right lane, but the car sped past her. She kept her speed intact for the next two exits and got off at the Old Milton Parkway exit. With a few more turns, she was at the gate of the exclusive Country Club North subdivision. The gate was wide open, and the security guard wasn't at his quarters. Zola sped through and headed straight toward the Benjamins' opulent estate.

Police cars were everywhere. Zola parked her car and jumped out. As she was running up the driveway, she saw Carmen being led out in handcuffs.

"Where is my son?" she screamed at the redheaded lady.

"He's my son. You're unfit ghetto trash," the woman said, "and you'll never get him back."

Zola ran after the woman. A police officer tried to grab her, but she slipped past him. She reared back and punched the white woman in her temple. She swung again, catching Carmen in the back of her head as she went down. The policemen who were holding her saved her from smacking her face on the driveway. A skinny rookie officer, who looked like the comedian Carrot Top, ran over and restrained Zola. He threw her to the ground, placed his knee on the small of her back, and slipped on the handcuffs.

"Let her go," a voice said.

Zola turned her head and looked into the face of Detective Shilo.

"Sir," the officer pleaded, "I just witnessed her assault that woman."

"I said let her go," Shilo repeated.

The officer removed the handcuffs and stood up.

"Help her up," Detective Shilo said. "And apologize."

The officer frowned at him but did as he was told.

"I'm sorry about that as well," Detective Shilo said.

"Where is Jason?"

"He's fine. We have him down at the station. Unfortunately, we can't get in touch with the judge right now, because he will have to lift the temporary order."

"Well, what's going on here?"

"Your friend Andy, aka Andre, spilled the beans. He was working for the Benjamins. Their plan was for him to woo you until you trusted him enough to commit a crime for him. Once that crime was committed, you were going to get caught and be sent to prison for a long time. Problem was, he started liking you for real and couldn't bring himself to do it. So they told him—"

"Wait a minute. Did you just say 'they'?"

"Yes," Detective Shilo said, nodding his bald head. "Mr. Benjamin was in on it too. They offered to pay Mr. Dubois one million dollars for you to disappear. Didn't matter if he killed you or had you killed, but like I said, he really liked you and just couldn't bring himself to do it."

Zola was shocked and appalled all at the same time. "When can I get my son?"

"I'm not sure. You should have your attorney look into that for you."

Just then, Mr. Benjamin pulled up to the front of his house in a white Range Rover. He was rushed by about five police officers. He stepped out of the car with his hands up and surrendered peacefully. Chad Benjamin made eye contact with Zola, and she gave him a look that could kill an elephant. Chad dropped his head and walked with the police to a waiting car.

"Thank you for all that you've done, Detective."

"Don't mention it," Detective Shilo said.

"Ms. Zaire," said Detective Sullivan, the rail-thin partner of Detective Shilo, walking up with his trusty notepad, "I have some bad news."

"Don't you always?" Zola said.

"Your mother set this whole thing up. She used to work for the Benjamins. This entire deal was her idea, but she had a change of heart and threatened to blow the lid off the whole deal, so Mrs. Carmen Benjamin had her taken out. I'm a little concerned right now because there is another target. I want to know if you can help me save this man's life. Who is Ian DeMarco?"

Zola was still stunned that her mother was connected to these people who were sitting in the back of police cars.

"Ms. Zaire?" Detective Sullivan said. "Stay with me now. Time is precious. We are trying to save a life."

"I never heard of that name," she said.

"Are you telling me the truth or are you following some street code?"

"Didn't I just tell you I don't know that name?"

"He's the man who took you to your mother's house. I have reason to believe that his life is in danger as well," Detective Sullivan said.

"Well, if you know who he is, why are you asking me?"

Detective Sullivan shook his head and walked off without another word.

Zola sighed and looked up at the huge white mansion. She shook her head at all that wealth and could only wish she had a fraction of it, but then she hunched her shoulders as she realized that her love was worth more than any amount of money. She turned and walked back to her car as Detective Shilo walked beside her.

"When is the last time you spoke with your brother?" he asked.

Zola stopped walking and turned to face the man. "Why?"

"I have reason to believe that maybe he killed the man who killed your mother."

"No," she said as she felt her legs get weak. The last thing she wanted to see was her brother shipped back off to prison.

"Nobody suspects this but me and my source. Rather than have him come down and turn himself in only to be released later because it's pretty obvious that it was a justifiable homicide, I think I'm going to keep my findings to myself."

Zola looked at the man and wanted to hug his fat neck, but instead she placed her hands on his and gave them a tight squeeze. "Thank you."

"Don't mention it," Detective Shilo said. "I'm serious. Don't mention it. Not even to him."

"You have my word on it."

Detective Shilo handed her a business card. "I'd like you to call me if you have any problems, Ms. Zaire. I'd like to consider myself one of the good guys."

Zola smiled and nodded. "It's good to know that the police force still has good guys."

Chapter 26

Ian got Zola's telephone number from Ravon and said his goodbyes. He walked back to his house just as an ambulance was pulling up. He paused on the front porch and turned toward the driver and pointed down the street. The passenger nodded, and they pulled off.

"Uncle Ian," KJ said, still shaken from all the gunshots, "I think I wanna go home."

"I don't blame you, man. Just give me a second to survey the damage and we can get out of here."

Ian walked into the living room and noticed three bullet holes right above the television set in the corner. He walked into Christian's room and stopped dead in his tracks. There was a bullet hole in his son's headboard. Ian walked over to the bed and ran his fingers along the wood. The hole was only inches away from his son's pillow. Ian looked up and saw something outside of Christian's window.

He turned on his heels and raced from the house. He jumped off the front porch and ran to the side of his house, where he saw Trudy lying on the ground. She was lying flat on her back with her eyes wide open. She was gone. Ian rushed over to the woman and leaned down. He felt for a pulse, but there was none there. He noticed that the front of her dirty shirt was red with blood. A bullet had caught her in the chest and probably killed her on impact.

Ian ran out to the street. He called out to the police officers who were still down at the end of his street. An officer came down.

"My friend is dead," he said as tears welled up in his eyes. "I couldn't find a pulse."

The officer ran around the house and dropped down to his knees. He immediately started CPR. He came up for air and used his radio to call for help. The ambulance backed up, and the paramedics jumped up and tended to Trudy. Ian gave them room to do their jobs.

Ian looked up to see Willie and Harry walking up the path that led to his house. For the first time since Ian had known him, Willie didn't have his sword. The old man looked at Trudy and burst out crying, his legs gave way, and Harry had to hold him up.

Ian shook his head as they loaded his friend onto a gurney and wheeled her out of his yard. Right before they put her into the back of the ambulance, he heard one of the paramedics say, "We got a pulse."

"Where are they taking her?" Ian asked the police officer.

"Grady. Do you know her name?"

"Trudy Blackwell. She used to be a doctor. Some kind of way she got on drugs."

The police officer shook his head. "That's such a shame. Here is my card if you need me."

"Thanks, but I think I'm moving out of here, man. A bullet hit my son's headboard. I couldn't live with myself if something were to happen to him."

"I understand that. You gotta do what you gotta do."

"Yep," Ian said and reached out and shook the officer's hand. "Thanks."

Ian stepped up on his porch and took a seat on the steps. Willie and Harry walked over and took seats too. They watched the chaos that was unfolding around them.

Police cars, ambulances, a chopped-up body, bullet holes, and near-death experiences were all a part of life in the hood.

"Fellas," Ian said, "I'm moving. Once I get settled into my new place, I will have you guys over for dinner."

Neither man acknowledged Ian's invitation. They were too lost in the moment.

Ian stood and walked back into his house. "KJ," he said, "I want you to go into Christian's room and gather up as many of his clothes as you can. We won't be coming back here."

Once they had every item Ian wanted loaded into the car, Ian walked back over to Willie and Harry. He reached out and handed Willie the key to his house. "Here you go," he said. "I need a favor. Once Trudy gets better, I want you to give her this key. You tell her I will be back over here to check on her."

"You a good man, Ian. A damn good man," Harry said.

"One of the best to ever put on a pair of pants," Willie echoed.

"Y'all not bad either," Ian said as he walked to his truck. "God bless ya."

"We gonna need it," Harry said. "We shole gonna need it, living around here. God bless us all."

Epilogue

"'Happy birthday to you. Happy Birthday to you. Happy Birthday, dear Jason. Happy Birthday to you,'" the crowd of about fifty people sang.

Zola was all smiles as she reached out and gave Detective Shilo a hug. He handed her a large, brightly wrapped box for Jason.

"I'm so happy you could make it," she said to the man who had been a blessing to her and her family. Ravon's role in the white man's murder was never mentioned, and for that, Detective Shilo had cemented himself as a true friend in her heart.

"It's been a long time. At least three or four months since I've seen you guys, right?"

"Yes," Zola said.

"Well, you are looking lovely as ever," Detective Shilo said, then turned to his left. "This is my wife, Donna."

"How are you?" Zola said, reaching out and hugging the woman. "Your husband saved my life."

Zola always gave Detective Shilo that credit because, without him, she may have been sitting in a cell right now as the Atlanta Police Department framed her just to close the books. It was his thorough detective work that put the right people behind bars. Shortly after all the walls came tumbling down on the Benjamins, the courts canceled Zola's temporary custodial release and placed Jason back in her care. Andre/Andy was sitting in a cell and would be there for a very long time for his role in the Benjamins' scheme.

"You guys make yourselves at home," Zola said. "There is plenty of food and punch."

"Thank you. But let me tell you," Shilo said, "your son is going to be an attorney. He's so smart. Without him, I'm not sure we would've gotten a conviction."

"Thank you," Zola said. "He's been skipped two grade levels already."

"I bet," the detective said.

"Do you need anything else, love?" Ian said to Zola. "I'm about to head downstairs to watch the game."

"With all this company in here?"

"Yeah," Ian said. "All of the guys are down there. Eagles and Falcons starts in six minutes. I already gave away my tickets. I'm not about to miss the game, too."

"Man," Willie said, walking into the kitchen area. He was cleaned up nicely but refused to take off his sword. "I need something a little stronger than punch."

"Hey, Willie," Harry said, motioning him over, "I found the stash. Come on."

Ian smiled and shook his head.

"Oh, Lord," Zola said. "You and your friends."

"Speaking of friends, look what the cat done dragged in," he said, looking at Walker and all his kids coming through the front door.

"Damn, Walker. What did you do, rent a minivan?" Ian said as he walked over and shook his friend's hand. He reached out and gave his wife a hug.

"Damn," Walker said, "I knew you was rich. Look at dis house. You holding out. Give me a job where you working."

"We'll talk about it," Ian said. "All of the fellas are downstairs, and that's where I'm headed too."

"You're wrong for that," Zola said.

Ian leaned over and gave her a kiss on her lips. They had been an item since his phone call to her on the day he moved out of his house in the West End. "But you're so right for me."

"Don't you try to butter me up, buddy," she said, pretending to be upset.

Ian shook his head as if he weren't falling for that one and made his way downstairs to their full basement. Andrea was sitting on the sofa, yelling at the television because the Eagles ran the opening kickoff back for a touchdown.

"Come on, Mom," KJ said. "Don't hate."

"KJ," Andrea said, "how can you be an Eagles fan when you were born and raised right here in Atlanta?"

"Two words. Mike Vick."

"Oh, hush," she said, still frowning.

"What's up, Pops?" Ian said as he plopped down in a chair beside his dad. "Are you okay?"

Colin DeMarco smiled. Christian was on the floor by his feet, playing with his cars, and the old man looked like he had died and gone to heaven. "I'm doing just fine. My son is living in a lovely home, he's back with the family business, and he has a gorgeous woman. Malcolm is running things on the West Coast, and Andrea is still fussing."

Ian nodded. "What more could you ask for, huh?"

"I can think of one thing: a beer," Colin said, and before he could finish his sentence, Willie handed him one from the stash he had in his cargo pockets.

"You're not supposed to steal from folks when they invite you into their home, idiot," Harry said.

"I'm not stealing. I was saving myself a trip to the fridge, stupid."

"Who you calling stupid, you ugly—"

"Oh, Lord," Ian said.

He turned and saw Jason staring at him. He stood and walked over to where the little boy was sitting all alone. "You don't like football, Jason?"

"No," he said.

"Are you enjoying your party?"

"Yes," he said, never taking his eyes off Ian's.

"What's wrong?"

"Do you like my mom?"

"I do. I like her a lot. I like you, too. Do you like me?"

Jason hunched his shoulders. "I'm not sure."

Ian frowned.

"My mom has been through a lot. My dad was an older guy who took advantage of her when she was a teenager. I read lots of stuff about her when I was living with the Benjamins. Stuff I probably shouldn't have read, but I did. She seems happy with you. You're the first person she ever wanted to be with. Everyone else she felt like she had to be with for whatever reason."

"Well, I'm very happy to hear that she wants to be with me. I want to be with her too."

"She doesn't need a boyfriend who will up and leave in a few months. She needs to stay happy forever."

"I can do my best."

"Do you know what I realized?"

"What's that, Jason?" Ian asked.

"My mom is the best mom in the world. She let me go live with some strangers because she loves me more than she loves herself. She's the prettiest woman in the world, and I don't care what I read in those papers. She's pure as the driven snow. My momma's a virgin."

Ian smiled and rubbed Jason's head.

"I couldn't agree more, son. I couldn't agree more."

Also available in August 2023

Black Hamptons

by

Carl Weber

with

La Jill Hunt

Carolyn Britton

1

I stepped off the elevator on the 36th floor in a black Armani silk blazer and pencil skirt, Manolo Blahnik heels, and the red Hermes scarf that made me feel powerful whenever I wore it. Behind me were my pride and joy, my two handsome sons. Malcolm, the oldest, was tall, lean, and quite brilliant when it came to business. His younger brother, Martin, was muscular, athletic, and especially easy on the eyes. Unlike his brother, who was more of an introvert, Martin was a true people person. He could charm the panties off a nun if he had to, which could be useful when it came to closing deals.

"Mother." Malcolm gestured toward a row of benches, where Jeffrey Bowen was seated. He was married to my niece, Leslie, and he was also our family attorney. He jumped up from his seat the moment he saw us, closing the gap between the bench and the elevator in five long strides.

"Aunt Carolyn." He kissed my cheek, then nodded at the boys. "You're right on time. Follow me."

Jeffrey led the way through double doors and into a small courtroom, where a middle-aged African American judge sat on the bench. I had to stifle the urge to call out, "Hello, Robert," reminding myself that we were in his courtroom, not at one of the numerous dinner parties in the Hamptons we'd both attended over the thirty years that I'd known him. Judge Terry, however, didn't seem to have any trouble separating business and pleasure. He kept his head down and didn't acknowledge me in any way as we took our seats at a table facing the judge's bench.

"Mr. Bowen, as the attorney of record for Amistad Bank, I see that you have made a motion. Would you like to elaborate?" Judge Terry spoke formally into a microphone, still not even glancing in my direction.

Jeffrey rose to reply. Like his father and grandfather before him, Jeffrey was a highly respected attorney. His practice was mainly in New York, but he had also spent time working in the office of the White House legal counsel during President Obama's second term. "Your Honor, we move that the conservatorship of Amistad Bank be removed and that the Moses Britton Trust be turned over to Carolyn Britton and the Britton family, so that Mrs. Britton's status as acting chairwoman and CEO of Amistad can be made permanent. Thank you, Your Honor."

Judge Terry placed his glasses on his head and began thumbing through the paperwork on his desk. After a minute, I started to feel restless. He was taking way too long for my taste, especially considering the fact that the outcome of this little horse and pony show had been determined weeks ago over drinks at my summer home in Sag Harbor. Judge Terry, along with a few key Democratic figures, had agreed to release the conservatorship in a wink-wink, nod-nod agreement. In exchange, Robert's son would receive a one-percent interest rate on a mortgage for a summer residence next door to the judge, and some up-and-coming Democratic candidates would receive generous campaign support from the bank.

"Any objection from the government, Mr. Lee?" Judge Terry glanced over to our right at Matt Lee, a small, well-dressed Asian man. He was a pain-in-the-ass federal banking regulator, and he sat next to Sara Wilson, an assistant deputy U.S. attorney.

"No, Your Honor," Mr. Lee replied. "The Brittons have met all the terms of our agreement."

Judge Terry removed his glasses and closed the folder. "Then I see no reason not to grant your motion, Mr. Bowen. The conservatorship over Amistad Bank is hereby relinquished and returned to the Britton family, along with all assets belonging to the Moses Britton Trust. Good luck and godspeed. Case dismissed." Judge Terry slammed down his gavel.

"Thank you, Your Honor." Jeffrey turned to me, offering his hand. "Congratulations, Aunt Carolyn."

"So, that's it? The bank is mine?" Although I knew this proceeding had merely been a formality, it felt good to finally be over the finish line. After four years of Donald Trump's government trying to take what was ours, I had struggled to believe we'd ever get full control of the bank again.

"Well, technically it belongs to the family trust, but you run the trust, so yes, the bank belongs to you. That's what your husband wanted, for you and your boys to have the bank and continue his legacy."

"Well then, Jeffrey, you don't deserve a handshake. You deserve a hug for a job well done." I wrapped my arms around him and squeezed him tightly. This had been a long time coming.

Jeffrey turned and shook the boys' hands, then we exited the courtroom and got back on the elevator. Down in the lobby, we were greeted by Kimberly Simmons, our family's chief of staff. I admired Kimberly, whose rare combination of stunning beauty and whip-smart intellect was sure to take her far in life. She was just starting to come into her own as a businesswoman, and my plans were to one day have her marry my son Martin whenever he finally grew up and stopped hoeing around.

"Well, I assume from all the smiling faces that things went well?" Kimberly had a naturally happy energy about her, although when she had to, that girl could be a shark—which was why I liked her.

"Phenomenal," Malcolm replied. "Jeffrey got the regulators off our asses, and now we can get back to making real deals instead of all this small business loans shit."

"SBLs and minority loans have been the backbone of Amistad since its inception, Malcolm. Never forget where you came from, son, because when you do, it will bite you in the ass every time. I promise you that," I replied.

"You're right, of course, Mother. I'm just looking forward to doing some big money deals like Daddy used to," Malcolm said.

Malcolm had always been a daddy's boy, and his dream was to one day run Amistad like his father and grandfather had. He had the brains for it, that I could never deny, but he hadn't proven he had the balls for the job yet. I guess now that we had full, unregulated control over the bank again, time would tell.

"Malcolm!" A familiar voice interrupted us.

We turned our attention to David Michaels, a wiry, brown-skinned man who made his way excitedly across the lobby. He gave Jeffrey, Malcolm, and Martin brotherly handshakes then turned to me and gave me a quick hug.

"How are you doin', Mrs. Britton?"

David came from an old money family that had made their fortune in construction and real estate during the seventies. He'd attended Hampton University and graduated at the top of his class in accounting, passing the CPA exam on his first try. The man was a whiz with numbers. My husband, Moses, had tried to recruit him to work at the bank when he graduated, but surprisingly, David had declined. He accepted a job offer from a big white accounting firm instead. I swear, sometime these young people think the white man's ice is colder.

"I'm doing fine, David. What brings you to the federal courthouse?"

"I'm with my boss, filing patents." He turned around and spoke to a man seated on a nearby bench. "Hey, Anthony. Look who's here!"

I watched as the man rose from the bench. If this was his boss, then it appeared David had left his job at the white accounting firm. This man was tall and handsome, with a smooth milk chocolate complexion. There was a woman with him. She was good looking also, although her too-tight outfit detracted from her overall look. If he was the boss, he should consider asking his secretary to dress a little more professionally.

They approached us, and David made the introductions.

"Mrs. Britton, have you met Anthony and Sydney Johnson? They live a few doors down from you in Sag Harbor."

So she was his wife, not his secretary. I couldn't help but let out an accidental chuckle when the girl reached back and pulled an obvious wedgie from her skirt. The men didn't hear it, but she sure did, and she shot me the most evil look in response.

Oh, well. Too bad, honey. Next time wear something a little more appropriate.

Anthony offered his hand. "We've met briefly at one of the homeowners association meetings, Mrs. Britton. Nice to see you again."

"Ah, yes. The new owners who bought the Petersons' house. You're the tech guy, aren't you?" I said. I must have met him soon after he bought the house, but he couldn't have made much of an impression on me, because the memory was quite vague.

As he shook my hand, I looked over at his wife again and got a good look at her dress, which, in addition to riding up her backside, revealed too much cleavage to be considered tasteful. From the cut and quality, I guessed it was an off-the-rack find from some mid-range mall store. I was not impressed. From what I understood, her husband's tech company was extremely successful, yet she dressed as if she were married to a manager at Best Buy. Poor thing probably didn't know any better, though. I wouldn't be surprised if he'd met her on Instagram or maybe even at a strip club.

She narrowed her eyes at me slightly, as if she could feel me judging her, so I slowly let my eyes return to Anthony Johnson's face. He was smiling at me.

"The tech guy. Yes, some people do call me that," he said.

After Jeffrey introduced Anthony and his wife to my sons, he announced, "Well, ladies and gentlemen, my job is done, and I'm going to take my leave." He gave me a quick hug. "Hopefully I'll see you folks out east this weekend?"

Since it was Memorial Day weekend, the official start to the summer season in our beloved beach community, I would normally have already been out there preparing the house for weekend guests, but I had one more task to complete before I could go. I'd had Malcolm call a special meeting of the board of directors in anticipation of the judge's ruling. I couldn't wait to see the surprise on their faces when half of them found out I was replacing their disloyal asses. Only after that was complete would I be able to relax and enjoy the opening of summer in the Black Hamptons.

"We'll be out tomorrow," I replied. "Your wife has me helping out with refreshments for the HOA meeting. I'm making crab cakes."

"Well, I was supposed to go sailing," Jeffrey said with a grin. "However, if you're making crab cakes, perhaps I should reschedule."

"Perhaps you should."

"We're going to take off, too, and see if we can get ahead of some of the traffic," Anthony said as he took his wife's hand. A look of relief passed over her face, as if she was pleased to be getting away from us. "See you in the Black Hamptons."

Anthony Johnson

2

"What's the matter? You still upset about Carolyn Britton?" I glanced over at my wife, who had just let out a long sigh.

"You didn't see the way that woman was looking at me, Anthony." Her voice was starting to take on that Brooklyn edge that always crept in when she was annoyed. "She was looking down her nose at me."

"Syd, what does she have to look down her nose at you about?"

Despite her annoyance, she gave me the cutest smile. "You know, for a man so smart, you can be so naive sometimes. Women like Carolyn Britton don't need a reason to be petty. It comes naturally," she replied just as I slammed on the brakes to avoid a car swerving into our lane. "Watch out, babe!"

"Look at this jerk!" I yelled, tightening my grip on the wheel. "Dude! You're not gonna get there any faster."

"God! I can't believe this traffic," Sydney groaned, fidgeting in her seat. "How long until we get there?"

Sydney hated riding in a car. Anything over forty minutes and she would be shifting in her seat like a little kid. My Sydney was a city girl through and through, born and raised in Brooklyn and proud of it. She preferred the bus or the subway, although she tolerated the drive from the city to Sag Harbor because she loved our home on the water so much. Normally we could make the trip in two hours, but it was the Friday before Memorial Day weekend, and traffic was backed up like a son of a bitch. We'd been on the road almost four hours, and Sydney was about to lose her mind.

"It'll clear up once we get past the Southampton split," I replied.

"And how long is that going to take?"

"Maybe twenty or thirty minutes." I glanced over to see her arms folded and bottom lip poked out. It was pretty obvious she was about to have a tantrum.

"What's wrong now?"

"I'm bored. I'm tired of being in this car, and I'm horny as hell. You didn't finish what you started this morning."

A smile crept up on my face. This morning was pretty special, or at least it had been until a call from an important client interrupted us. When you own your own business, sometimes you have to make sacrifices to keep things running smoothly, and that includes answering phone calls even when you're busy trying to get it in.

"I know, and I'm sorry about that, but what was I supposed to do, Syd, miss Victor Singh's call? But we can take care of that as soon as we get to the house."

"I'm horny now, Anthony," she snapped.

"Syd, there's nothing I can do right now for you. We'll be home in a bit, and I will service all your needs. I promise."

"Hmph. Maybe there's nothing you can do now,
I'm a take charge kinda girl." She turned to me wi'
devilish smile, then unhooked her seat belt. Sydney
hiked up her dress and slid off her panties, spi
them on her fingers sexily. I swear my wife knew
fuck with me.

"Are you trying to make me run off the road?" I

"Keep driving. You ain't seen nothing yet."

I glanced over to see what she was doing and h
a double take.

"Are you . . . are you masturbating?"

"Yup."

"You can't wait until we get home? Traffic's s
move."

"Nope. I've been in this car almost four hours
and I'm bored as shit, so keep one eye on the
the other on me so you can watch the show
kept doing her thing like I wasn't even there.

"How many times do you think I can make m
before we reach the house?" She let out a l
and I exhaled, shifting my eyes every few sec
the road to my sexy-as-hell wife. Her perform
woken the other Johnson in the car, the one be
legs.

Twenty minutes later, I was still fully erect, a
had taken the liberty of releasing me from
and giving me a massage. By the time we pu
neighborhood, I was the one squirming in m
to lose my mind.

"What the fuck?" I snapped as we turne
block, which was more crowded than I'd eve

"What?" Sydney lifted her head from my
over the dashboard. "Where'd all these
from?"

ooks like someone's having a party," I replied as I
red at the rows of cars parked on both sides of the
et.

o?"

't know, but it better not be our kids."

and I had two college-aged kids, a son, Tyler, and
er, Gabrielle. They'd come home from Virginia
iversity a couple weeks ago and headed straight
each house. Now I wondered if it had been a
to let them stay out there by themselves until
l Day weekend. They were good kids, but they
kids.

and I adjusted our clothes. As we got closer
use, I could hear the music booming so loud
ny closed windows that it sounded like it was
car with us.

ed as nervous as I felt. "Anthony, I hate to say
might just be our kids," she said. There were
ple who looked to be in their late teens and
ties headed down the block in the direction of
e.

r not be," I growled.

ulled up in front of our driveway, I realized
that the teens were walking past my prop-

's a relief. It looks—"

bitch!" Sydney yelled, interrupting me.
that? Those little shits ran over my gera-

good thing is the party is not at our house.
t's over at the Brittons," I said, trying to
tive as I pulled into our driveway.

Just as I'd feared, though, Sydney was not going
be placated. "I don't give a shit. I just planted th
geraniums. It took me two days to put those th
in," Sidney said, stepping out of the car to inspe
flowers.

By the time I got out of my seat, she had alread
her phone out of her purse and was dialing.

"What are you doing?" I asked as I approached

"I'm calling the cops."

"For what?"

"For my geraniums. Those things cost like e
dred dollars," she said angrily.

"Put the phone away, Syd. I'll buy you so
geraniums."

"I don't want you to buy me more flowe
not the point," she said. "I spent two days
putting those flowers in, and you can't giv
that time. Some little bougie-ass kid just tr
over my flowers, and I want someone to pa
disrespect."

"Babe, I know you're upset, but stop and ti
minute. I don't want the police in front of my h
flashing lights over some flowers."

Sidney lowered her phone, giving me a lool
tion and understanding.

"Maybe we could just go over there and
Brittons," I suggested.

She paused, and for a minute, I thought
then she smiled devilishly. She lifted her
and pressed the button to make the call.

"What are you doing?"

"Calling the police." She chuckled.

"Why?"

"I don't want the police in front of our house either," said. "But I do want them in front of the house where e noise is coming from. The house with rude guests uin my flowers."

l, that's a bad idea . . ."

was already talking on the phone before I could ny sentence.

'd like to make a noise complaint."

s too late to stop her, but I knew without a at my wife had just opened up a big-ass can of